"In his latest epic, *Beyond Human*, author Ken Decroo introduces us to a riveting tale of government shenanigans and man's struggle to better understand his closest relative in the animal kingdom. Decroo—thanks to his years of expertise as an animal trainer for the movie industry—provides piercing insights into the behaviors and thought processes of the great apes as well as our fellow human beings, with sometimes unsettling results. And then … what about bigfoot?."
–**John Russell, author of *Riding with Ghosts, Angels and the Spirits of the Dead* and *A Knock in the Attic*.**

"*Beyond Human* is the third offering in Kenneth L. Decroo's riveting series about super-powerful human-chimpanzee hybrids being developed by a shadowy government agency as super soldiers. Turner's efforts to get to the bottom of Vandeussen's plot are complicated by the local belief that the legendary bigfoot lives in the area. His belief system is turned on its ears when he experiences the eerie forest firsthand, and in Decroo's hands so will yours be. This is a book that you do not dare put down until you reach the end. Masterful execution and outstanding storytelling."
– **Charles Ray, author of over 40 books.**

"Another page turner! They thought life had returned to normal, but little did Dr Turner and his crew know, Vandusen and his gang were up to their evil and sinister ways. Vandusen is motivated by fame and fortune, but this time his evil is driven by revenge against Turner. What fate awaits the chimps Danny, Oliver and Girlie? Are the creatures truly monsters or is their behaviour justified? This story has a twist you won't see coming?"
–**Joanne Larsen, BS natural science & education director at a zoo.**

"Wow, what a capstone to this amazing, thrilling trilogy. Well worth the wait, Beyond Human continues the excitement, intrigue and solid biomedical foundation, finally intertwining it with American folklore. I couldn't put it down."
–Tom Bachman, Research Faculty, School of Biomedical Engineering, Czech Technical University, Prague.

"Once again, Kenneth L. Decroo has kept me on the edge of my seat and left me wanting more. Beyond Human finds Drs. Ken Turner and Fred Savage at a crossroads. Chimp hybrids are roaming Africa and, most likely, somewhere in North America. The DOD is building a remote experimental station, and a group of campers are found brutally murdered. Filled with plot twists and the cross-continent connection of mystery and subterfuge the group of scientists and their guides need to find answers. The conflicts that arise are met by rugged determination of these men to protect humans, the creatures, and the secrets from the jungle. Another thriller by a masterful storyteller."
–Jamie S. Morris, English teacher.

"Where do I find the words to tell you how much I enjoyed this book? What an incredible story. The characters, the tension, the plots and sub plots, bad guys chasing good, descriptive international characters and locations adding into the mix, the knowledge and behavioral studies you share, the depth of the love and respect described between animals and humans, the dramatic and intense climax to the story all kept me engaged from the very start.

When I closed this book, at the end, the characters stayed with me for several days and even as I write this. I want more of Oliver and Girlie... Your book is truly amazing."
–Gary Seiler of Gary Seiler and the Coast Riders, musician.

BEYOND HUMAN

Kenneth L. Decroo

AIA PUBLISHING

Dedication

*To my loving wife, Tamara Lynn Decroo. You keep asking me
to tell just one more story, so I keep writing.
I love you.*

Chapter One

The Eureka Courier
May 21, 1985
Willow Creek, CA

FAMILY OUTING ENDS IN TRAGEDY!

Willow Creek mourns the loss of several of their own. Four families were brutally attacked by unknown assailants in the early morning hours of May 10th at a popular campground in the nearby Shasta-Trinity National Forest. In addition, six teenage girls are now missing from the campground.

National Forest Ranger Lt. Jim Kelly reported, "I've never seen such a brutal attack in my thirty-two years as a patrol ranger and tracker. It was worse than anything I ever encountered in Vietnam."

Lt. Kelly reported he stumbled onto the scene while tracking a wounded black bear. He stated that he initially thought the victims had been mauled, but soon realized "a wounded bear isn't capable of such a savage attack."

Authorities are stumped as to who or what perpetrated this horrific massacre, and more importantly, what has become of the missing teenage girls. The Humboldt County sheriff has assigned Lt. Kelly to lead the search and hopefully rescue them.

Many in the community are doubting their own safety as they speculate on who could have perpetrated such a horrendous act, ranging from Charles Manson-like cults to the creature locally known as Bigfoot.

Ironically, Willow Creek depends on Bigfoot tourism and bills itself as the "Bigfoot Capital of the World," holding an annual Bigfoot Daze parade. It even houses a Bigfoot Museum in a local hardware store.

Several townsfolk stated they believe Bigfoot exists and that the creature is gentle and reclusive, and not capable of such a brutal, savage act.

Is this a change in the behavior of the town's favorite "gentle giant of the forest?" Only time will tell as the tourist season approaches and the good people of Willow Creek prepare for this year's Bigfoot Daze.

***

Ranger Jim Kelly of the US Forestry Service took measured steps through the jagged rocks. He'd been hiking on the high ridge above the timberline all afternoon searching for clues.

Who massacred those families and abducted those teenage girls? He stopped several times and leaned over, hands on his knees to catch his breath. He had to press on. The thought of those young girls being held captive by who knows who or what was unbearable. He knew the families of many of the teenagers. His own daughter would've been on that family outing, had it not been for cheer camp.

The sun beat down on his shoulders. He knew from experience this relentless high-country sun could burn him right through his khaki shirt, but he had to keep searching. Soon he'd have to make camp for yet another day.

He'd been the first to discover the savagery and couldn't forget that horrible day when he'd stumbled upon the gruesome scene. *How long has it been? God, almost a month already.*

He remembered when the massacre first hit the wire services. It'd been chaos in their little community. The news media had swarmed into town and camped out in and around the crime scene for weeks. But when nothing more had turned up, most left as abruptly as they'd come, seeking more sensational news, and leaving the leaders of the little town to pick up the pieces while Kelly tracked the perpetrator.

The Humboldt sheriff gave him the less glamorous but meticulous task of sorting through the wreckage of the campsite—the crime scene—for clues. The savageness of the attack and the mauled remains of the bodies had unsettled all involved in the investigation. Even the troopers sent over from Sacramento and Portland, who were used to the most ghastly crime scenes, had been taken aback. He remembered one young trooper who'd no sooner arrived on the scene before he pushed his way past everyone and heaved his guts out.

Usually, Kelly felt at peace when patrolling these stands of old-growth trees, but not now. He was on edge. The dismembered corpses he'd discovered at the campground sparked flashbacks of Nam. Now he sensed something had changed in the woods. He felt a menacing watchfulness he couldn't explain. Possibly just his imagination, but he felt it just the same.

He quickened his pace as he picked his way along the spine of the ridge, trying to get a better vantage of what lay behind and beyond the meadow where the families had been attacked. He was trying to reach higher ground, and it had taken him all day to climb to this outcrop. The trail, if you could call it that, was getting harder to follow as he navigated through the rocks. The soil was furrowed, so he couldn't find any distinct footprints, only broken branches and disturbed ground. Something large had plowed its way up the slopes.

He wasn't sure if he was even following the right trail, but he had to continue no matter how hard it was. He was still hopeful, though. Tracking and scouting were what he did best. Despite his title, he was a tracker more than a ranger, and he preferred to work alone. Kelly loved the straightforwardness of his work. It was always the same routine: work with the sheriff to find clues, pack up, and track. He loved the chase, had used his skills many times to help solve crimes, and was the first choice of the local law. But up until now, he'd chased and caught petty poachers or fugitives, mostly. Searching for these girls was different. These youngsters were friends of his daughter. He knew their parents and had watched them grow up. Yes, this was different.

Too many gawking outsiders, more interested in the gory details of the attack than finding the missing girls, had shown up and muddied the waters. At the town hall meeting, the mayor had assured the townspeople they were safe. But Kelly wasn't so sure. The mayor hadn't seen the carnage he had.

Kelly frowned, accentuating the wrinkles that creased his leathered face. He couldn't shake off the effects of the murder scene. The images had taken root in his psyche. He paused, his short, compact frame stiff as he remembered it all. He'd been following a wounded bear a hunter had reported when he stumbled upon the campsite in the meadow. At first, he'd thought the shredded and dismembered bodies were the work of the bear, but a wild animal wouldn't commit wanton and cruel mutilation like he'd found, no matter how wounded and in pain. The scene was as grisly as anything he'd experienced in war. And like those flashbacks that visited him from time to time, he would have to try to file them deep into the backwaters of his subconscious—but not just yet. He'd have to live with this nightmare and make an uneasy truce with those unnerving images for as long as it took to find those girls.

Finally, he shook himself loose from those dark thoughts and continued to scramble up the rocky spine until he reached a lone stunted cedar that struggled to grow in a clearing of crumbled, decomposed granite. He'd gone at least a mile without a single track or sign revealing itself.

He paused and sipped from his canteen as he readjusted his pack. He wiped his forehead with his bandanna, absentmindedly scraping his boot on the clearing's coarse granite—the worst ground for tracking. In widening circles, he walked the entire knob of the hill looking for signs, anything that would show him the way. Still no clues. He climbed up on the boulders and looked in the cracks for anything that might have been dropped.

Nothing, a goddamn dead end.

"What now?" Kelly shouted to the empty wilderness. His voice echoed off the surrounding peaks, interrupting the brooding silence. As expected, only the wind answered him in gusts. From high on the ridge, he could see the whole valley below. The thin green ribbon probably marked a creek running out of a thicket of trees. He nodded and spurred into action, making his way to that cluster of trees. He'd need to hurry now. Daylight was burning.

He refused to return with nothing to show, leaving no hope for those poor families. He had to stick to it. He'd double back and try another route. Perhaps he'd missed a turn, a jag, and overshot their trail. At first it had been so clear, as though whoever or whatever had no fear of being followed. That was unnerving.

He scrambled back down until he reached the base of the

ridge and struck out toward where he thought the creek lay. He'd have to depend on his intuition now, working on luck and guesses—even his own footsteps didn't leave tracks in this crumbling granite. He pressed on until he reached the creek, a tiny ribbon of water so small he could hop over it. But someone or something hadn't hopped—they'd stepped carelessly into the moist mud at its edge. The impression of a large footprint, partially filled with water, pointed the way. Several more imprinted the soft mud leading up the creek toward the thicket. For sure he'd picked up the trail again. The size and nature of the huge, humanlike prints shocked the ranger. Though larger than his own, they were definitely feet—just not human. The depth of the impressions indicated that a large creature had made them.

He'd heard rumors and stories of Bigfoot sightings for years, but this was the first evidence he'd encountered that made him wonder. It was hard to deny his own eyes. The size and shape of the footprints were similar to castings he'd seen in a local hardware store in Willow Creek. A logger in the early '50s had made casts of several tracks he'd found in his logging camp. He'd reported to the local sheriff that his camp had been vandalized and several huge oil drums thrown into a ravine. These reports, and the castings of the footprints, had set off a flurry of newspaper stories.

Several years ago two men from the Willow Creek area claimed to have filmed a bigfoot in a meadow not far from where he stood. He'd watched the film when the two men, Patterson and Gimli, had shown it in a local high school auditorium. The creature's realistic movement had shocked him, but he'd wondered if it wasn't just a well-designed hoax. Hoax or not, the film had been shown around the world and had set off a scientific controversy.

Until now, Kelly hadn't believed these creatures existed,

always thinking them a ruse, probably perpetrated by kooks and nuts looking for their fifteen minutes of fame and a payday. However, these footprints unsettled him. He'd tracked long enough to know the difference between prints made by a person with a fake mold and ones made by a living creature. He'd once tracked a runaway who'd attempted to fool him by using plaster of paris molds. He recognized at once that they were fake, static. These prints were left by a foot that moved and flexed—not made by a rigid mold. The toes were in different positions and the heel prints sank to different depths. These were real and not like anything he'd ever found in these woods. Though not human, they were humanlike. From his experience tracking, he'd seen the tracks the bare feet of humans left. They had a longitudinal arch—an upward curve that ran from the ball of the foot to the heel. These prints were flat, showing a more flexible midtarsal joint. Most striking, the toes were proportionally longer, taking up a bigger percentage of the foot.

When he pulled out his camera and crouched down to get closer look, a musky, pungent odor assaulted his olfactory sense. It reminded him of a pile of dirty, wet diapers, only worse. He bent over, retching from the smell, only to realize it wasn't coming from the track, but instead was being carried downwind from the nearby thicket of cedars. He pulled his small measuring tape out of his pocket and measured the print. Seven by sixteen inches. Leaving the tape for scale, he took several photos of the footprint, knowing he'd need them to be believed. He didn't want to be ridiculed and grouped with all those Bigfoot cranks. If it weren't for this investigation, he'd probably keep this discovery to himself. He might still.

The gusts that always came with sunset were just starting to freshen. He stared, but his eyes couldn't penetrate the thicket's shadows. Just as he was about to look away, he thought he saw a slight movement. Hoping to preserve it so he could make a cast later, he carefully covered the track with pine needles, then set out toward where he thought he'd seen something.

His hard-earned instincts made him cautious as he pushed up the creek toward the thicket. His path would be easier now. He had only to follow the disgusting scent. He quickened his pace and tracked, almost at a run now, following his nose—until something caught his eye that froze him in his tracks.

Chapter Two

Dr. Ken Turner stared at the blinking light on his office phone. He wasn't sure what was more irritating, the damn blinking light or the loud ringing. Since his return from their adventures in Africa over a year ago, every time a phone rang or he heard a knock at the door, it startled him, bringing back memories and—even worse—nightmares of the creatures. He and his colleagues had been able to settle back into their old lives and a semblance of normalcy. But they were not without a feeling of dread. The contrast between what they'd gone through and the quiet university life they lived now set an ominous tone that filled every part of his life. Ken wondered if the others had the same feeling. He hadn't been in touch with his friends down in Southern California much since he'd returned to the States.

Someone must know I'm in here, or this damn ringing would stop. He took a deep breath, pushed the button, and answered. "Dr. Turner speaking."

"Ken, it's Mark. I just heard from Lt. Sandy."

Ken realized that he hadn't seen or heard from the detective since they'd returned. He exhaled before asking, "How's he doing?"

"Never mind that just now. Can you meet at Frank's?"

The old feeling of dread swam over him. He'd been waiting for the other shoe to drop for months. But just enough time had passed that he almost felt like his life might continue without Vandusen and his thugs and the Department of Defense. He cleared his throat and tried to keep his voice level. "When?"

"I'll send you some newspaper articles that should interest you and check to see when Fred is back from the field—a week or maybe two, at the most."

It was always hard to read Mark's dry English manner, but Ken thought he could detect tension in his voice. He hesitated before he asked, "What's this about?"

"Not on the phone. I'll be in touch."

An abrupt click followed by a loud, irritating dial tone ended the call. Ken held the phone away from his ear. *Shit. I'd better call Mary.*

Ken's wife, Mary Turner, was the only person who could keep him grounded when he was stressed or experienced a "red alert," in Mary's words. As a Hollywood film director, she was used to dealing with the chaos of a movie set. She'd been the only person able to keep Ken from spinning out of control when everything had unraveled.

***

The morning shift was in full swing at Frank's Bar. The bartender, Scotty, and a young barmaid were busy cleaning up from the evening shift. Scotty concentrated on drying beer mugs by alternating between wiping them on a dish towel and the front of his T-shirt. His tall, lanky frame contrasted with his petite assistant. The barmaid entertained the clientele by reaching up to the shelf above to stack plates. Her tight halter top drifted up, revealing her thin, athletic waistline. A few warehouse workmen, who sat at a worn Formica counter hunched over steaming breakfast plates, enjoyed the show. Streams of light sifted through the sagging venetian blinds, faintly highlighting faded murals depicting grander times for the little bar.

Three men and one woman sat in a corner booth nestled in the back, next to the bathrooms. Their scholarly demeanor and dress seemed out of place among the blue-collar workers just off from the night shift.

"So what do you think?" Dr. Fred Savage asked as he dropped a folded newspaper into Dr. Ken Turner's outstretched hand. Fred brushed back his thick red hair to expose his pale, freckled forehead before he reached for a frosty mug.

Ken frowned and lowered his voice. "It looks like the *Sacramento Bee* reran this from the . . . *The Eureka Courier.* Where the hell is Eureka?"

Even sitting in a booth, Ken's tall, lanky frame towered over his companions. Not waiting for a reply, Ken put on his reading glasses. His hazel eyes scanned the article while Fred looked around at the others and motioned them to wait for the professor's reply.

Finally, after he had reread the short article twice, Ken wriggled out of his corduroy sports jacket and said, "This is not good. Bad. Really bad. And Bigfoot? Really?" He poured the last few dribbles of Hamms into his glass and looked around before shouting to the bartender, "Another pitcher, Scotty!"

Scotty smiled from behind the counter. "Coming right up, professors. You'll have to pick it up yourself, though. We're swamped up here." Scotty handed the barmaid a tray of steaming burgers and pitchers of beer and pointed toward a group of off-duty police officers playing pool. He looked back at Ken and shrugged.

Ken smirked, taking notice of the almost empty bar. He

nudged Consuelo Leon, who sat beside him, to retrieve the pitcher, ignoring her grumblings about the plight of lowly grad students. He admired her gracefulness as she glided across the room. A dark-eyed, shapely beauty, she was one of his smartest students and had been a real asset to the whole team in Africa—a real star. Nevertheless, she was willing to humble herself and pay her dues to her major professors. He remembered his own serfdom as a grad student at Berkeley, right down to mowing the lawn and washing the car of his senior professor every week. He leaned toward Fred and asked in a hushed voice, "So these reporters actually think it's Bigfoot who massacred those families?"

Fred nodded. "That's the gist of this article, and not too subtle, I might add. The fine folks at the *Courier* apparently know what sells."

"I'm not sure if that helps or hinders us," Dr. Mark Chaney whispered, knowing their voices would carry in the empty room. His English accent always drew attention in these American bars. A few workmen occupying the next booth attended to plates of eggs and chili chased by frosty mugs of beer and were engrossed in their own conversation about union matters. Mark smiled and thought how similar Frank's was to the places back home in Kent. Like the neighborhood pubs of England, there was always a small clientele who chose their favorite local establishment over going home after the night shift. He was struck by how empty Frank's felt in the morning compared to evenings, when he usually visited. He and his colleagues would need to be more discreet.

Consuelo sauntered back with a pitcher and, with a final glare directed at Ken, slid into the booth next to Mark and poured before she spoke. "Well, it's obvious what killed those men and women and kidnapped those little girls. It sure wasn't any creature like Bigfoot." She winked her left eye slightly as though to punctuate "Bigfoot."

That subtle blink of her eye was a habit that Ken, like most men, found very alluring. It wasn't a flirting wink in this context, but more like how you'd point your finger to emphasize something. He thought what an attractive couple his two young assistants made. Mark's refined manner and movie-star looks had made him very popular with the college ladies—almost too popular. And Consuelo's fiery persona and striking features had captivated Mark like many before him. The trials of the last couple of years had bonded all of them together, not just Mark and Consuelo. He realized that though they'd all been drawn closer in spirit since Africa, their little group of conspirators was scattered all over the country.

Ken pulled himself back to the conversation. "I agree with Consuelo. We've all seen this handiwork before."

Nodding, Fred leaned forward, catching their attention. His chiseled face wrinkled as he whispered, "It's Africa all over again . . . I know what you're getting at—the creatures."

The group sat deep in thought, oblivious to their surroundings, until the bright morning light streamed in when someone opened the front door. They could just make out the silhouette of Lieutenant John Sandy. He slid into their booth and dropped a newspaper on the table before he spoke. "Sorry I'm late."

Pushing the paper aside, Ken said, "We've already read this. I guess the Reno Sheriff's Department gets the Sac Bee as well. Mark shared this with me."

Sandy paused, smiling at all of them. The last rays from the closing door highlighted his blond hair. His blue eyes took in everything around them. The group had learned it was an ingrained habit that kept Sandy's edge and situational awareness.

It'd paid off many times on their adventures, especially in Germany and Steinwasen Park. "So what do you think?" Sandy asked.

"Well, it's good to see you as well!" Ken replied before continuing, "I think we need to take a trip to the little town of Willow Creek and have a chat with the ranger mentioned in this article. It seems he gets around the area a lot." He shook the paper.

"Yes, Willow Creek," Sandy said as he reached for a mug. Holding it and motioning to Consuelo, he asked, "Do you mind?"

Before she could respond, Ken reached in front of her and filled Sandy's mug. Ken waited for everyone to settle, then said, "Let's examine what we know. We lost Vandusen and his crew in Rotterdam, where we're pretty sure they left with some of the creatures headed to parts unknown—somewhere in the Pacific Northwest, I think." He picked up the newspaper and began reading in a whisper, "Willow Creek mourns the loss of several of their own. Four families were brutally attacked by unknown assailants in the early morning hours of May 10th at a popular campground in the nearby Shasta-Trinity National Forest." He paused to clear his throat. "And it goes on about how important Bigfoot is to the community, blah, blah, blah."

Consuelo frowned, pushed her silky black hair from her face, and interrupted. "I have to agree that this smells of Vandusen and his people. Maybe even Dr. Melon." She nodded to Ken. "I've been doing some reading since Sandy shared this article. What I've found is that sightings of Bigfoot have been reported across the Pacific Northwest for centuries but rarely associated with this kind of violence. Almost always, the accounts describe them acting defensively and trying to escape. I remember watching a film a few years ago from an expedition of supposed Bigfoot researchers. The animal was shy and made a bipedal retreat.

From what I've read, most scientists don't believe they exist. They consider it some kind of hoax." Consuelo paused and picked up the newspaper. "If Bigfoot populations exist, they've managed to evade detection by hiding, not attacking. This massacre is too much like what we experienced in Africa. Don't forget what those sadistic gangsters did to us there. They managed to destroy a lifetime of research on hybrids that the Belgians had conducted, not to mention attacking and destroying their facility. Those people are intent on killing everything in their path. We still don't know who's funding this madness. Forget Bigfoot. It's more likely those gangsters have somehow lost some of the creatures we think they kidnapped, and if that's so, they'll change the whole narrative in this part of the world. This is just the beginning."

"I hate to say it," Sandy said between long gulps, "but this Bigfoot thing could work to our advantage."

"What do you mean?" Mark asked. He noticed Sandy was showing the first signs of graying, mostly around the temples. This whole adventure had affected them all in one way or another.

Sandy picked up the empty pitcher. "As Consuelo just mentioned, it will change the narrative. It might serve as a distraction and keep prying eyes off us if we went up there and poked around."

"Perhaps," Ken said as he slid his empty mug back and forth on the table. "But this incident is going to bring every crazy Bigfoot hunter from around the world, besides the law, to that little town. We'll be tripping over them."

"What if those creatures really exist?" Consuelo asked.

Ken's brow furrowed. But before he could reply, Fred cut him off. "So we're going to be 'tripping' around up in Willow Creek?" He smiled when he noticed the beige arcs worn through the red Formica. Apparently rubbing beer mugs back and forth had been a habit of countless patrons at Frank's—a historical artifact of people worrying. He stood to fetch another pitcher as his friends sat in silence.

Sandy broke the silence, saying in a whisper, "Well, I have some interesting information that might be helpful, since we're talking about Willow Creek."

"And what would that be?" Ken nodded at a group of students who passed their table. Frank's had begun to fill up.

"As you know, Melon is a person of interest to my department, and we've been trying to locate him. He's been missing since before we left for Germany." Sandy pulled out a small, frayed notebook from his back pocket. They waited as he flipped several pages. "Here we are. Let's see . . . According to his past employer at the National Science Foundation, or the NSF as you people call it, he's turned up near that town of Willow Creek."

Ken frowned. "That can't be a coincidence, and it explains where he went after he supposedly 'retired' from the National Science Foundation and his duties reviewing my signing chimp research here in Reno."

"In my line of work, I don't believe in coincidences." Sandy pulled his sweater down to cover the butt of his .38 service revolver.

Ken nodded. "Nice sweater." Before Sandy could respond, he continued, "I wonder what would bring Melon up there, so far away from anyone whose ass he could kiss."

"Apparently, you're behind the times, Dr. Turner. I think your focus on your chimps has put you out of touch with the latest breaking news." Sandy paused for effect. "There's a new primate center being built by the Department of Defense in the Pacific Northwest, near Willow Creek."

"And Melon's going to work there?" Ken asked.

"Actually, he's going to run it," Sandy replied. "He'll be the senior research scientist. The DOD has moved his whole family up there. It looks like they'll be living in style at the new facility."

"Run a primate center!" Ken emptied his mug and slammed it down on the table, drawing attention from the next table.

"Easy, Ken," Sandy said as he looked around at the adjacent tables.

Ignoring Sandy, Ken's voice rose. "This makes no sense. Melon would be in way over his head." He shook his head. "I'd like to see that."

Sandy nodded. "Exactly, so let's go see. Let's head up there."

"How are we going to do that and not run into Vandusen?" Ken asked. "I don't think we want to end up guests in that facility. We've been there and done that—don't forget Africa. I bet Vandusen can't be far away, and he and his men are the last people any of us want to see." He looked around nervously.

"With everything going on right now, I think we'd just be another group of outsiders, and with all the law enforcement crawling around, I think Vandusen will be laying pretty low," Sandy said. "We could blend in, get lost in the crowd, if we assume the cover of Bigfoot hunters. I could check in with the local law and represent myself as a fellow off-duty officer assisting you scientists." He picked up the newspaper. "We'll make them believe our presence isn't related to what just happened to those families."

"And Vandusen and his thugs?" Ken asked as he absently rubbed a scar that ran like a crease on his cheek. He often joked that it was a dueling scar, but actually it was from a chimp encounter that had gone wrong.

Sandy's blue eyes darkened to almost black. "You let me handle that." He pressed his lips together.

Ken thought better of asking how Sandy planned to handle Vandusen and changed the subject. "So you really think we could blend in up there?"

"Right now, yes. Have you ever seen the aftermath of one of these fiascos?" Sandy continued to leaf through his notebook. "Every law enforcement and news agency within a couple of hundred miles will be crawling all over each other and that little town. This is the perfect time to do some recon."

Ken smiled. "And we wouldn't want to miss Bigfoot Daze."

"Bigfoot what?" Sandy asked. He smiled and continued, "I must have missed that tidbit in my investigation."

"Days, spelled D-A-Z-E," Ken said. "The whole town devotes three days to their famous celebrity: Bigfoot. Hell, they even have a parade. It's the perfect time to go."

"Will they have it this year, considering what happened?" Fred asked.

Ken nodded. "The festival and its parade are a big part of the town's economy. You can bet they will." He tilted his head. "I've been doing some research of my own concerning that little town and its economy."

"What about the rest of the group?" Mark asked, looking at Sandy.

"Lester's in LA with Girlie. I know he worked with Dusty and Chris at the Wild Animal Training Center for a little while, but I'm not sure what he's doing now. Bobby's on a show and being Bobby, which is a full-time job. Hunt has disappeared somewhere in the Castro district. I'll try to contact them all. I think we're going to need them real soon." Sandy made notes while he answered.

The group emptied their beers almost in unison and cleared the table of their belongings.

Scotty watched Ken and the rest as they filed out. Leaning over to the barmaid, he whispered, "I wonder what they're up to now. Trouble seems to find those guys everywhere they go." He remembered an evening not so long before when they'd fled for their lives, leaving Frank's in wreckage. He shook his head and stuffed a washcloth into another mug.

The little group headed out the open door, shading their eyes against the noon sun.

The barmaid grinned at Scotty and said, "Dr. Savage is kind of cute."

Scotty sighed. "Come on, it's time to clean out the walk-in."

Chapter Three

Melon rocked back and forth trying to find the words to motivate the foreman who stood holding a clipboard. The glaring sun beat down, baking the yard's red clay. Melon squinted as his headache began to throb. To make matters worse, clouds of mosquitos descended on his pale, sunburned skin like the dinner bell had just rung. He pushed his wire-rimmed glasses back up the bridge of his hooked nose and patted his head with a large paisley bandanna to mop his thinning hair, which matted in dark, moist clumps. The professor was losing the battle against sweat dripping down his nose. Even his wife had said he looked sickly and had a pasty pallor.

The air felt heavy. The sweltering heat and no breeze made this the worst time of the day. Later it would be just the opposite as the fog rolled back in from the distant ocean. He hated the outdoors. His short, portly frame wasn't built for stomping through undergrowth and climbing over logs. And the work! The work had been slower than he'd anticipated, and the general had left unhappy. His parting words hadn't been good. He'd threatened to call up Vandusen to help "motivate" him to get the creatures settled in and begin what he referred to as a proper training regimen.

Melon didn't like the idea of Vandusen and his thugs coming to "motivate" him. And worse, he was beginning to realize what the general meant by *regimen* and was horrified by the prospect of working with those freaks. They were huge and aggressive—monsters that had the worst traits of both humans and chimpanzees. But he was more horrified by what would happen if he couldn't carry off the training.

Despite the heat, Melon felt a cold chill. Why couldn't these thugs grab that asshole Dr. Turner and drag him and his lackeys up here? The general could force them to have this disaster up and running in no time. And if he could convince Turner to start playing ball, they could all get rich.

He looked around the abandoned logging camp they were converting. It was a mess. Piles of wood chips, rusting equipment, and stacks of timber clogged the clearing, making it difficult to move around. The forest and valley walls seemed to close in on all sides. It was a dark and dirty place. Even worse, occasionally something stirred in the old-growth trees surrounding them, unnerving even the mercenaries working for his "employer."

He'd rushed to get the caging in place, but the fencing slowed them down now. The men had managed to string it up in some places, but in other spots, they'd had to cut their way through the dense thickets of trees and undergrowth. There was much still to be done. To further complicate matters, he hadn't been able to bring in enough local contractors, his job made harder by the need for secrecy. Worse, he couldn't instruct the few workers he'd been allowed to hire on what they were building, which left him in charge of design.

Melon swore under his breath. The general just didn't understand his predicament. He was a research administrator, not some kind of construction manager. The general had never grasped what his role was in the scientific community. He evaluated other scientists' research after they'd designed and built their own goddamn facilities. Then there were the cries he and his family had to endure, day and night, from those abominable creatures. Only four of the beasts remained, the others lost in the plane crash, and they couldn't be sure where they were now, although Melon felt they'd survived and lived close-by in the forest. Patrols went out every day searching for the creatures they'd managed to lose. All anyone had to do was follow the news to know those ungodly creatures were out there somewhere. Fortunately, the best thinking of the local yokels was that Bigfoot, of all things, had attacked those families a few weeks ago.

He realized the foreman was still waiting for instructions. Frowning, he said, "Just do the best you can."

The foreman exhaled. "If I knew exactly what these cages were for, I'd know how to mount them."

"Just secure them like goddamn King Kong himself is going to be in there."

The tall man looked down at Melon, speechless for several seconds, before he sighed and walked away muttering to himself.

***

Nothing in the facility seemed to be finished. Dr. Melon looked at the spreadsheet he'd so meticulously crafted and realized nothing had been checked off. He muttered under his breath as he approached a crew of workmen stretching wire on the perimeter fence.

"How much longer?"

One of the men looked up from his work and shrugged.

Melon shouted up at them, "I need this whole fence finished by tomorrow!"

"Then give us more men and start delivering the materials on time," the foreman said, bristling.

Melon opened his mouth, but seeing all the men getting up and clenching their fists, he thought better of saying any more. Instead, he turned and walked toward the main caging.

Several of the men glared and gave the universal finger gesture.

One of the men hissed, "Knock it off! Do you want to get us all fired?"

"That idiot can't fire us. He's way behind schedule. He's the one who's got to worry about getting fired. He's clueless." Shaking his head, the foreman yelled to one of the men below the scaffolding, "Hoist up another roll of goddamn wire."

Two men lifted what looked to be the last roll.

Melon stopped in the middle of the yard to survey the haphazard piles of lumber and building materials. He watched as several men dug through the piles looking for more wire. It was no wonder the workmen couldn't find what they needed. Worse, the locals he'd paid to clean up the timber and debris had left it in shambles. That would be the last time he'd pay any of these local yahoos in advance.

"It's hopeless!" he yelled, ignoring the workmen's looks. His voice echoed off the rocky walls of the valley. Several of the workmen looked up and shook their heads again before returning to their work.

A dark foreboding had come to visit him. He wished he'd never met that shit Gordon Childs and his so-called friend, Vandusen. He wasn't sure how he'd managed to dig himself and his family into this hole, and, more frightening, he didn't know how he could get out. He was in the middle of nowhere with a bunch of gangsters. The nearest town with a real university was hundreds of miles away, and worse, there was no real law and order anywhere near them.

He and his family were prisoners in this godforsaken armpit. Thinking about it now, he should've just left Dr. Turner alone and moved on back to his quiet life on the East Coast. Now he was in real trouble. The general was expecting results, and he couldn't give them. He'd observed in the last few months that it wasn't healthy to let the general down. He wondered who the man really was. Hell, he didn't even know his real name. Everyone just called him "the general."

He thought his mood couldn't get any worse, but his heart sank when several Land Rovers raced into the yard and sped to where he stood, stopping in a cloud a dust.

Melon froze as several men dressed in military fatigues climbed out of their vehicles. They surrounded the lead vehicle and stood waiting as the driver stepped out and opened the passenger door. Melon's blood ran cold when his eyes met Vandusen's.

Vandusen paused, sneering at Melon, before he slammed the door and picked his way toward him, his tall, lanky frame casting a long shadow against the setting sun. He tripped over the scattered debris and swore. "This place is a clusterfuck! What the hell have you been doing for the last two months?"

Melon had to concentrate to decipher Vandusen's thick accent. *Was it Eastern European?* Vandusen didn't have to say a word to frighten him. He had dark, menacing eyes and the bearing of an SS gestapo officer you might see in the movies. Melon realized he needed to stop thinking along those lines and say something.

But before Melon could answer, several of the men in fatigues surrounded him and shoved him in the direction of a small shed across the yard. Melon had wondered what was in that shed and unfortunately realized he was about to find out. The workmen stretching the fence seemed amused at the contrast between the tall, lanky Vandusen and the short, portly Melon.

"Looks like our little Napoleon is in Dutch with his boss," the foreman said, laughing. The workmen watched Melon disappear into the shed.

The door shut with a clang, surprising Melon. Bars lined the inside of the corrugated-iron office.

Vandusen smiled as Melon watched one of his men slide a padlock through a latch on the bars with a snap. "A little trick I learned from our colleagues in East Berlin. There's only two ways out of here now, Dr. Melon."

Melon tried to swallow several times, but his mouth was too dry. "Two ways?" he managed to ask.

Vandusen nodded to the man standing by the door and said, "A glass of water for the professor, if you please. Yes, two ways. But we're getting ahead of ourselves."

Melon could barely hold his glass steady enough to take a sip. More ended up on the floor than he managed to drink. He looked around at the men surrounding him, but before he could speak, Vandusen continued, "The general's not happy, and I think you know what that means."

Melon tried to speak, but Vandusen waved him off. "Unfortunately, we're not in the market for excuses. The general has asked me to take over this operation, which leaves you to me."

"Me?"

"Yes, you. The general is thinking maybe we don't need you anymore. From the looks of this place, I'm inclined to agree."

"I tried to tell him, the general, that I don't know anything about construction and building primate facilities."

"That's obvious."

"If you could give me and my family transportation to the airport, we could be out of here in less than an hour."

Vandusen and his men chuckled and shook their heads.

"You don't get it, do you?" Vandusen lowered his voice.

"Get what?"

"Your contract with us is for life." Vandusen glared and his face tightened, accentuating his high cheekbones and giving him a sinister appearance.

"But—"

"Right now, I'm trying to figure out how long you have left on that contract."

It took a moment for the last statement to sink in. Melon realized that what he said and did in the next few minutes meant life or death for him and his family. He froze when one of the men started picking through a pile of tools on the workbench. The man finally settled on a hammer.

Melon couldn't take his eyes off the hammer as the man softly tapped it in his palm. The man met his eyes with a cold stare and then looked at Vandusen.

Vandusen shook his head and whispered, "Not just yet. Let's weigh Dr. Melon's options."

"Please, just let us go. We won't be any trouble. We won't say a word." Melon's voice quivered.

Everyone but Melon broke into laughter.

The man with the hammer sneered and said, "For an educated man, he sure is a slow learner."

He stepped forward, but Vandusen held out his arm to stop him. "Not to worry, Dr. Melon. As I said, we're not going to do anything to you just yet. I'm thinking we should get your family more involved. Maybe we should organize a little coming-out party for that teenage daughter of yours. I think the men would really enjoy that."

Melon's vision narrowed, and he had trouble catching his breath. His legs felt like they'd give out. He grabbed the back of a chair to steady himself and tried to control his voice. "Please, just say what you want. I promise I'll do it, anything. Just please, leave my family alone."

Vandusen sneered. "Well, that's really more of the spirit we're looking for. You need to take more of an interest in getting this goddamn mess cleaned up and finished. The general thinks you need to put more of your heart into this project. That's why he asked me to motivate you. So what do you think? Are you motivated yet?"

Melon nodded his head and whispered, "Yes." His mind raced and his heart pounded as he imagined Vandusen and his men manhandling his family. His daughter.

As though reading his mind, Vandusen's eyes locked onto Melon's. A chill passed over Melon as Vandusen's eyes turned black and cold. "I'm not sure I heard you."

"Yes!" Melon shouted. His voice bounced off the corrugated metal walls of the shed. His eyes welled up, making it hard for him to see.

Vandusen slapped Melon on the back. Laughing, the other man set the hammer down.

***

It was evening when Vandusen and company left the shed. He looked around in the darkness, doing a mental inventory of what was needed before they could move the creatures into their new caging. The general had made it very clear he wanted the training to begin ASAP. But his military training made him equally concerned with erecting a secure perimeter fence around the camp.

Melon's an idiot, Vandusen thought.

He grabbed ahold of one of his men who was passing and ordered, "Find Bauer." The man nodded and raced off without a word.

A few seconds later, Bauer arrived, still tucking in his shirt.

"There's no time to catch some Zs. We've got work to do. Gather the men and set some lights up."

"Sir?"

"We're going to stretch some wire and finish the goddamn fence. Get all the rolls of wire you can find in this mess." Vandusen pointed toward the shed. "And get all the M18 Claymores we have left. I want you to set a minefield all along the fence line."

Bauer frowned. "Shall we rig them with trip wires?"

Vandusen shook his head. "No! Do you want some pain-in-the-ass local hunter tripping them off? We'll have to trigger them remotely, so we know who we're welcoming."

Bauer smiled at the prospect. "I'll get the men ready."

Vandusen put his hands on his hips, surveying what needed to be done, and said, "You have two days before the general returns."

Bauer mimicked his boss standing with his hands on his hips. "Can do, sir."

Vandusen looked Bauer up and down for a moment, then ordered, "Carry on!" Just as Bauer turned, Vandusen stopped him and added, "We're gonna need to get rid of these locals before we move the creatures out in the open."

Bauer nodded and raced off without a word.

Vandusen no sooner gave the order than there was a flurry of activity in the yard. Groups of men scurried from pile to pile, locating and dragging material to staging areas. He admired Bauer's precision.

Bauer can be a complete idiot when it comes to seeing the subtleties of a good plan—the big picture. But he's hell on wheels carrying out a direct order.

Vandusen made a final turn around the area and was pleased. With Bauer on the job, they'd have this place ready for the general's inspection, but he wasn't as sure about the condition of the creatures. He didn't have a clue how they were going to get those monsters out of the travel cages and into the new breeding cages they were finishing. And it was becoming quite clear that that idiot Melon didn't either. If the general hadn't said they needed Melon as a frontman, that little shit would be lying in a shallow grave already. He needed to convince the general to pick up that bastard Dr. Turner. It was time he renewed his interest in the good professor and his people. He'd speak to the general. They needed to kidnap Dr. Turner and company and bring them up here as their "guests." Vandusen's lips drew back, and his face hardened at the prospect of hosting Dr. Turner and company. He smiled and mouthed, "Payback's a mother . . ."

He stopped to watch a crew building scaffolding out of timbers that cluttered the yard. Very efficient.

Looking around at all the activity ramping up, it was obvious he was just in the way. Bauer was in his element and wouldn't stop, day or night, until the job was finished. He exhaled and paused a moment, looking up the drive. The lights were still on at Melon's residence—not that it mattered. He smirked and decided it was time to pay the family a visit, especially that young teenager Melon seemed so desperate to protect.

Chapter Four

Kelly stooped to pick up a tennis shoe, a girl's gym shoe, small and pink. He thought it out of place in this wild, lonely place and didn't want to think about who'd dropped it and why. He turned it over and rubbed the sand off the canvas. It hadn't been there long. Obviously, its owner had gone to great lengths to make it her own by drawing hearts and flowers on the canvas with a blue ink pen. The laces were looped two eyes at a time, separated by a crisscross pattern, like his daughter and her friends were in the habit of making. He searched for more traces or signs, but the ground was too hard even in the creek bed. He circled the creek for several yards but found no more clues, so he decided to keep following it toward the thicket.

He stopped, hesitant to enter, and examined a large limb lying at his feet. It seemed odd there, so he stooped to pick it up. It still had fresh green leaves on it. He fingered the frayed but sharp splinters where it'd been broken. It didn't look like a typical windfall. That usually happened to dead branches and had a clean break at the end. The wood fibers between the splinters were frayed as though something had twisted and pulled it apart. He racked his brain trying to think of any animal that would do this.

He slowed his pace to take in the edge of the dark, foreboding patch of cedars. A breeze picked up and hissed through the branches. The shadows of the dense stand made it hard to see beyond the first line of trees. He could just make out, at the edge of the forest line, a string of saplings bent over to the ground. He couldn't reach where they curved down but guessed the bends to be about fourteen feet high. All limbs seemed to be pointing in the same direction, out and away from the rest of the trees. He'd never seen large saplings bent down like this and wondered what could've done this at such a height. They seemed to mark a boundary, and he was reluctant to cross it, sensing something or someone lurking in the darkness. Feeling a chill creep up his back, he unslung his Savage 30-30.

A musky smell clung to the breeze as he stepped under the overhanging limbs and entered into the darkness. He stood for a moment to let his eyes adjust. At first all was silent. He listened for any movement but only heard the creaking of the windswept treetops. He looked from side to side, hoping to pick up a path, but the dense vegetation hemmed him in. Just as he was about to stoop under some low-hanging branches, he heard a piercing whistle followed by the crack of what sounded like a large tree limb breaking. Loud hollow tapping, like someone pounding sticks against tree trunks, filled the forest. He froze when he heard what sounded like answering cries. The forest came alive with the echoes of whistles, cries, and limbs snapping. He couldn't see anything, but he heard rustlings in the darkness coming toward him.

He backed his way out into the open in a hasty retreat and looked back over his shoulder just in time to duck a flying boulder. Several more rocks whizzed by him, just missing his head as he took flight. He could make out movement in the shadows in the direction from which the projectiles flew. A deafening chorus of cries like he'd never heard before filled the valley, sending birds to flight. He ran back up the creek toward where he had found the tracks.

I'm gonna need backup.

Kelly had to get help and get it right away. Whatever was in the shadows of that thicket, he didn't want to meet it alone. He decided to make his way back through the meadow and head back toward the campground where this nightmare had begun. After the campground, he knew a shortcut that would get him back to town, where he could get help. He was going to need more guns to follow that trail any further. But before he left, he'd take the time to make a plaster cast of the print.

He was relieved when he found that the small ziplock bag of plaster of paris he always carried was still in tack and hadn't hardened. He smiled to himself. *Just like the Boy Scouts, "Be prepared."*

After digging a hole out of the mud to use for a bowl, he poured some water out of his canteen and used a stick to mix in the plaster of paris, slowing his stirring as the paste thickened. Then he dipped his stainless Sierra cup into the mixture and carefully poured it into the track. A few minutes later, it had hardened enough for him to lift the mold out of the impression. Now he had some proof, or at least he hoped it would convince the sheriff that he hadn't been seeing things.

He stood and looked back up the creek toward the thicket. Dusk was announcing the coming night. What were those ungodly sounds, and what the hell had made them? *They have to be connected to those poor girls' disappearance*, he thought as he closed and shouldered his pack.

Fortunately, a full moon had risen early and the sky was clear, so he had no trouble following an elk trail. It connected a chain of high-country meadows that the elk used every summer.

He felt tired and scared. Something was up here, and he was alone. He stopped to listen. Did he hear rustling in the meadow grass in the darkness behind him? Was he being followed? He couldn't hike all night. He needed nourishment and rest, but he didn't relish the idea of spending the night up here where he might meet god knows who or what. He hadn't heard any cries or whistles since he'd left the thicket, but he was sure something was nearby. He skirted the shore of a lake and was jogging toward another meadow when he tripped on something in the grass. He shone his flashlight on a large, jagged piece of metal, and walking through the knee-high grass, he found several more pieces of what looked like wreckage of an aircraft. He racked his brain but couldn't remember any reports of an airplane crash in this area. He'd have to wait until morning to go any further.

A grassy apron near the tree line looked like a good place to make camp for the evening, so he walked over and busied himself gathering dry leaves and sticks to start a fire. The first tendrils of the growing flames warmed and reassured him, and soon after, he had the soothing sound of his coffee pot perking and the aroma of the fresh brew. Some things never changed. A campfire and the smell of coffee always made him feel at home, even in the backcountry. The camp coffee, laced with some Wild Turkey, and the roaring campfire warmed him, but he kept his rifle ready. It was going to be a long night.

***

Kelly woke with a start. Despite the coffee the night before, he'd fallen asleep in the wee hours of morning before dawn. The first rays of the sun filled the meadow in a golden shower, but it didn't warm the chill. Birds sang to meet the morning, and he watched several elk grazing on the other side of the glen near a small stream. All seemed normal as he broke camp, until he saw the wreckage that the darkness had hidden. The tangled debris of what appeared to be a small airplane lay strewn across the meadow.

The grass had already begun to swallow the jagged pieces of the wing and fuselage. What appeared to be several large steel cages lay bent and tangled on the ground—puzzling—and flies feasted on what looked like splatters of dried blood. It appeared that the wreckage of this crash hadn't been here for very long. Yet he'd heard no reports of this incident. He turned a wing over, found part of a number and copied it into the notebook he carried in his pack. The whole scene unnerved him, as he couldn't explain how and why what remained of this plane had gotten there.

He'd need to return with the crew from the crime lab to find out what had happened. *Possibly drug runners*, he thought, *but what about those cages?* The meadow was finally warming up, and he was hungry. He'd make some oatmeal before heading for home. As the water heated on the campfire, he crawled into the fuselage, carefully took some scrapings of what he thought was blood, and found several patches of black hair.

A bear? he wondered. He didn't think so. It was too tight for any respectable bear to squeeze into. He took several samples of the hair, putting them into evidence envelopes.

When he heard his water hiss into the fire, he crawled out, planning to have a quick breakfast and hump it home. He still had a way to go, and he wanted to leave the high country before another night caught him. Something wasn't right. He could feel it. The quiet of the meadow unnerved him more than the cries he'd heard the day before. It was a brooding silence. Even the birds had stopped singing. Not for the last time, he felt he was being watched, maybe even being stalked.

He packed his gear without washing it, feeling an urgency that bordered on panic. It was time to go. He headed out toward the safety of home.

Chapter Five

"Willow Creek? Where in the hell is that?" Ken's wife, Mary Turner, stood glaring at Ken.

The rest of the group looked from one to another and then to the back door. Mary, being a famous film director, was used to getting her own way, and all who knew her, especially Ken, knew he was on a dangerous path right now. Besides that, she lived up to the stereotype of a red-haired, Italian-Irish woman. Her temper in Hollywood was legendary, and none of the crew wanted to be on the receiving end.

"Yes, it makes sense. There's a good chance Vandusen has managed to lose some of the creatures in the wilderness that surrounds that town." Ken's voice was strained as he looked past Mary in an attempt to catch Detective Sandy's eyes.

Mary searched the faces of the group and settled on Ken. "So is this Fred's bright idea or yours?"

Everyone looked from one to another, and finally Fred broke in. "Detective Sandy here thinks Melon may be up there running some kind of half-assed chimp facility. We think it's probably a cover for the DOD, the Department of Defense."

"I know what in the hell 'DOD' stands for."

Ignoring Mary's histrionics, Sandy broke in. "Right now

everyone in that little town is focused on the massacre."

"I read about that." Mary voice lowered as she stood and stared out the bay window. "I hope we didn't have anything to do with that . . . that . . ."

"Right now the whole town is in the moment," Sandy said. "The place is probably crawling with media and law enforcement. It's the perfect time for us to blend in and do some poking around."

Mark and Consuelo looked at each other, trying to avoid Mary's gaze, but it was too late. She turned to them. "And you two? I thought I gave you clear instructions to keep Dr. Red Alert from getting into any more adventures."

They knew that when she referred to Ken's episodes as "red alerts," she was either angry or worried, and there was no use trying to reason with her. They looked to Fred for help.

Fred tapped his pipe in his palm, nodded to Sandy, and said, "Don't look at me. You can blame this all on the good detective here."

His brow wrinkling, Sandy picked his words carefully. "Thanks a lot, Fred. We need to find out what Vandusen is up to. Don't forget, I still have a deputy missing, even if we think we know what happened to Dr. Melon. That missing deputy brought me to all of you, and it appears you have some nonhuman beings, or creatures, as you call them, missing as well."

"I wouldn't say *we* have any of them missing. We didn't spirit them away. But the fact is there are creatures missing here and in Africa, and we still haven't had much time to study any of them or, more importantly, protect them," Turner said.

They waited for Mary to reply as she turned to face them. The light streamed in, backlighting her amber hair and shapeliness; even in anger, she moved with gracefulness. Beyond the confines of the living room, through the bay window, they could see a chimp ambling down the gravel driveway with his human companion, or HC, as they referred to the handlers.

Finally, Mary said, "If you're set on going, I'm coming with you. You'll need someone with brains in this little operation of yours."

Sandy opened his mouth but before he could reply, Ken broke in. "I'm not sure what you mean by 'Dr. Red Alert.' If anyone has a calming effect, it's me."

At first everyone waited for Mary to explode, but she broke into laughter instead, followed by everyone else—everyone except Ken, who sat frowning. Mary shifted his mood, as she always did, by gliding over to kiss him on the forehead.

Ken looked up at Mary, stroked her cheek, and said, "I think I'll have a chat with that HC. I don't like how tight he's holding the lead on that chimp out there."

Mary kissed him again and whispered, "Don't be too late."

***

The cart rattled as Mary rolled it across the living room's shag carpet, being careful not to spill the contents piled on its glass shelves. A carafe of coffee, cups and saucers, plates, and heaps of scones slid around as the small rollers bogged down in the deep pile. The group looked up from their conversation as Mary began filling cups, and a rich aroma of roasted beans filled the room. They'd debated well into the evening, trying to come up with an appropriate cover that would allow them the freedom to move around the little town of Willow Creek, but at the same time, allow them to blend into the crowds that were apparently still up there investigating the massacre.

Mary smiled, watching each of her guests try to balance a cup in one hand and a plate piled with scones with the other while trying to return to their seats. *My god, they're hopeless*, she thought, then broke into the conversation with an idea. "I think Detective Sandy's plan of searching for a missing person has merit. It would explain his presence, but I think we need more to explain why the rest of us would be up there."

"So what's your suggestion?" Sandy asked.

Mary grinned. "Bigfoot."

"What in God's name are you talking about?" Ken asked as he stepped back into the room.

"Well, if you think about it, from the articles we've been reading tonight, the whole town in some way or another is connected to Bigfoot. Whether they believe in it or not, they certainly seem to be profiting from the idea. And even better, the media is suggesting that Bigfoot is responsible for the massacre. If we show up representing ourselves as Bigfoot researchers from a bona fide university and interested in joining the search, we—"

Ken interrupted. "You can't mean you want us to join the ranks of those kooks. We might as well look for UFOs while we're at it." Coffee spilled down his leg.

"That's fine, if you think that will give us free rein to poke around. If we have the blessing of the city fathers, we can wander almost anywhere and question whoever we want."

Before Ken could respond, Sandy broke in. "Actually, she has a good point. We'd each have a reason for being up there, and I'd make sure to keep my distance from you guys in public."

Mark walked over to the window, admiring the sunset against the Sierras, and said, "If you'd asked me if chimps could possess language before we began our work, I would've said no. And remember, it wasn't that long ago that we would've questioned the existence of human-chimp hybrids."

"I see what you're getting at, Mark. But really? Bigfoot?"

Ken joined him at the window. The others sat deep in their own thoughts.

Fred waved Sandy off as he went to speak. "Why not? Not everyone involved in searching for them is a kook. There are some genuine researchers who've at least suggested the possibility of their existence."

Ken frowned. "Like who?"

"John Napier, for one," Savage answered as he left the window and returned to the cart to refuel.

"Dr. Napier of *Homo habilis* fame?" Turner asked.

"The very same, Ken. Apparently, he began looking into the area when a film was released which claimed to show a bigfoot in the wild near, of all places, Willow Creek. Supposedly, the film captured a large, female bigfoot walking up a river wash. I remember having a brief conversation concerning the validity of that film over drinks with Jane Goodall at the American Anthropological Association conference in New Orleans. Now remember, this was over drinks, but she felt while much of the so-called evidence of Sasquatch was obviously a hoax, there was much that was inconclusive. She wasn't ready to rule out its existence. I believe, even now, she has an open mind on the subject."

"I need to see the clip of that film," Ken said. "I have to say, I'd need some convincing." He looked around the group. "So what do we do?"

"Our homework," Mary replied. She picked up the phone and motioned to Mark. "Do you have the number for that pretty librarian who was so helpful when we had Yuri over to translate those letters and photos that Bobby Waiter found in Mexico? You know, before we left for Africa?"

Mark looked from Consuelo to Mary, hesitating, before he said, "I'm not sure who you mean."

Mary put the phone down and smirked. "Come on, Mark. Have you gone brain-dead? The one you used to date when you first came here from England."

Consuelo stood and joined Mary. They both waited.

"Oh, of course. I remember now. I'd forgotten all about her."

"I see. Could you try to rack your brain for us?" Mary smiled at Consuelo.

"She works at the main library in the reference section, I believe," Mark answered with a slight quiver.

"You believe? We know that. Do you have her direct number or not?" Mary asked, pointing at the phone.

"I might just have it in my wallet. Let's have a look, shall we?" Mark began sorting through scraps of paper and tattered business cards. He gave a sidelong glance at Consuelo. "Gosh, I need to clean these old numbers out. Really don't need them anymore."

Consuelo watched every move that Mark made, staring at him with her dark eyes.

"Well, of all things, here it is," Mark said, handing the card to Mary. They couldn't help notice his trembling hand as he continued, "Fancy that. As I said, I really need to clean this out." Mark set into a flurry of activity, organizing his wallet while being careful not to make eye contact with anyone.

They all had to work to not smile. Obviously, Mark had been at his games again, and anyone who knew Consuelo knew he was in a real predicament—one that could end up being very unhealthy for him. Everyone knew she had a temper and easily became jealous. But no one felt sorry for him. This wasn't the first and probably was not the last time for Mark—that is, if he lived through this one.

Consuelo left the room without a word.

Mary sighed and said, "I think we should have Ken pay a visit to this cute librarian. Let's see, what was her name?"

She held the business card up to the lamp. "Ah, Tamara Dresden, Reference Librarian." She dialed the number, looking up at Mark with each rotation of the dial.

Chapter Six

Fred and Ken looked back at the house as they hurried down the gravel drive toward the chimp cottages. Ken smiled and said, "I wouldn't want to be in Mark's shoes just now."

Fred chuckled. "Mark has a way of getting into these jams wherever he goes. But to be up against Mary *and* Consuelo is not only daunting but downright dangerous." They both laughed.

Ken, in a more serious tone, said, "Then let's do something safer like visit Oliver and Danny."

Fred nodded. "Lead on, professor."

You could've traced their progress from just the hoots as they passed each set of chimps. Some were in their cottages while others were out for walks with their HCs. The men's progress slowed as they stopped to greet each chimp and their HC.

The two professors forgot their worries as they slipped back into the routine and rhythm of their research. The concentration it took to work chimps was a form of meditation. Ken had once said, in one of his lectures, that working with animals required seeing through the animals' eyes. Each species offered a window of perception that expanded our consciousness.

They heard Oliver and Danny before they saw them. Their greeting hoots were one of the only chimp behaviors they still possessed. Workmen had converted an old hay barn, left over from the ranch days, into a secret enclosure for them. It kept them safe from prying eyes. They'd built a large steel cage inside the barn for them with private den boxes for each. It was a temporary situation, but they weren't sure how temporary, as they had a dilemma. They needed to keep them safe and secret, but they needed to live outside, free, in the open forest. Ken and Fred had yet to solve this dilemma.

Danny and Oliver ran to the bars nearest to where Ken and Fred approached. Ken carefully handed them their favorite snacks, bananas. Oliver ate the first banana, peel and all, slowly spitting out the skin. Danny grunted as he carefully peeled his first.

"It's interesting how Danny eats his more like a human, whereas Oliver eats his like a chimp," Ken said.

Fred ignored him, intent on signing to both, "All good?"

Oliver looked up at him and signed, "Out now."

Fred answered with his hands. "Not now. Later."

Danny stood up and ambled toward them. Stopping at the bars, he signed, "Where Lester?" He made Lester's name sign, an L-shape with his thumb and index finger tapped against his shoulder. Danny had picked up sign language from the signing chimps that they'd brought to visit him on their daily walks with their HCs.

After slipping two boxes of donuts through the bars, while being careful not to get within reach, Fred signed, "Lester come soon, promise."

Both creatures signed, "Out, out."

Ken got up to leave and signed again, "Soon, promise."

Oliver whimpered, forming his lips like a trumpet.

Ken and Fred turned to leave as Danny and Oliver busied themselves opening the boxes of donuts. "We've got to find a place to set them free," Ken said.

They both walked in silence toward the playroom where they'd conducted the double-blind experiment so long ago. At least, it seemed like a long time ago.

"I hate keeping them caged up, but what are our alternatives?" Ken continued. "We had to take them out of Africa for their own good. The world is shrinking, especially over there. It's hard to believe, but that's how it is." He paused at the door to the playroom and looked back.

Fred nodded. "We need to find somewhere to release them where we can observe them adapting and living. Somewhere safe from encroachment."

They entered the playroom's observation booth, and Ken stopped, deep in thought. Fred waited for him to speak.

"What if we introduced them into the area where the massacre occurred? Do you think Oliver or Danny could have a positive influence on who or whatever massacred those campers?" Ken asked.

"Now that would be an interesting experiment, wouldn't it?" Fred said.

The door to the playroom opened and several chimps with their HCs raced in.

Both men laughed as they watched the chimps play chase in between picking up various toys that they named with signs when asked by their HCs.

"Let's get back to work and record some of this behavior," Ken said.

"With pleasure. God, I miss this . . ." Fred said with a sigh.

They picked up clipboards and pulled up chairs behind the one-way mirror.

For the moment, life seemed normal again. They nodded at Mark when he entered the room. Ken and Fred smiled at each other, noting the sheepish look on his face. They all settled into their observational work.

"Having trouble juggling your ladies?" Ken asked.

Before Mark could answer, Ken and Fred broke into laughter.

Ken marked boxes on the observation sheet. "Their vocabularies are definitely growing."

"Mary has kept the HCs at their work, thank god." Mark hung his clipboard on the wall and leaned back to watch the chimps play. The one-way mirror muffled their sounds, but the men could feel the vibrations of the chimps jumping from table to table as they raced after each other.

"I wish we had Lester and Girlie with us right now," Ken said, his voice wavering.

Mark patted Ken's shoulder and said, "We can call and get them up in no time."

"Do you really think so?" Ken's eyes welled up.

"Ken, what's wrong?"

"I don't like the thought of them alone in that dingy trailer after all we've been through together."

"You got room up here," Mark said. "Let's hire them . . . I mean, Lester as a consultant and set them both up here." Mark had never seen Ken so emotional and wondered if it was the strain of what they'd been through the past couple of years. Seeing his boss like that gave him an uncanny feeling.

Ken stood and paced the tight observation room before speaking. "That just might work. It wouldn't be charity, either. We could use his skills up here."

Mark nodded. "I'll make a call to Bobby and have him arrange it."

"Bobby Waiter! I miss him. What's he been up to?" Ken asked.

Fred smiled. "Working in Hollywood, as usual. We may not've heard from him, but I can assure you that he's been in touch with Lester. They're close. Always have been. I still remember my first meeting with Lester and Girlie in that little single-wide, like the odd couple, and Girlie smothering Bobby when he arrived."

They all laughed so loud that the chimps in the playroom ran up to the one-way mirror.

"Quiet!" Ken hushed them and handed Mark the phone. "Call Bobby."

***

Lester looked across the little kitchen table at the old chimp. "I wouldn't mind seeing Oliver and Danny again," he said into the phone. "Neither would Girlie." She tried to grab the phone. "Leave it!" he scolded.

Girlie whimpered, leaned back in her chair, and rocked.

"Sorry, Bobby," Lester said.

Bobby chuckled. "Great! Then it's settled. I'll send someone down to pick you and Girlie up. How soon can you be ready?"

Lester looked around his trailer. It had been lonely since his return. He pushed aside a pile of junk mail. That was all he seemed to get these days. He flipped through his calendar—all blank.

"Lester, you still there?" Bobby asked.

Lester leaned back as Girlie reached her hand out for the phone again. "How about right now?"

"Sounds good. The sooner, the better. I think Dusty's up for a little road trip," Bobby said.

"Here, say something to Girlie." Lester handed the phone to the old chimp.

She jumped up and down, hooted into the phone, and began smacking her lips.

Lester leaned closer to listen.

"Hey, Girlie, we'll see you guys soon. Okay?" Bobby said.

Lester had to admit, it would be great to see that pirate Dusty again. He'd worked with him and Dr. Chris Raven when they first returned from Africa. They'd had their differences over the years, especially after his wife, Karen, had passed, but he couldn't deny he'd been a loyal friend and a great help when they went to that dark little gypsy camp in the Black Forest.

"You still there?" Bobby asked.

Lester pulled out of his thoughts. Girlie still stood on her director chair and stomped her feet while she puckered her lips to make more kisses into the phone. She whimpered when Lester took it away. "Whatever floats your boat. Tell that bandit of a chimp, Mike, that I'll be up for some hide-and-seek." He glanced at Girlie and smiled. "Mike's the second smartest chimp I've ever known."

Lester hung up the phone, walked down the narrow hallway, and began to pack—a change of clothes and picture of Karen. He wondered what was next for them. They'd returned from Africa in one piece, but he had the feeling that their adventure wasn't over. They would, sooner or later, have to do something with Oliver and Danny. It was cruel to keep them caged, especially after their freedom in Africa.

But what and where? he wondered. He sat on his bed and patted for Girlie to jump up. Girlie hugged him as he stared into space.

Chapter Seven

The Congo, five months earlier

François grabbed his lieutenant's arm and whispered, "Get down."

After a month of fruitless searching, they'd ended up right back where they started. He, and what was left of his men, crouched, hunkered down in the tall elephant grass that filled the clearing which separated the caves from the jungle. He could just make out a band of creatures carrying what looked like fruit piled in baskets as they filed into the gaping mouth of a cave. A breeze hissed through the waving grass, obstructing his view with each gust.

He motioned to one of his men and ordered, "Give me your field glasses," but after a brief look through, he exhaled heavily, catching the attention of some of his men, and whispered to no one in particular, "These are no help. We're going to have to get closer."

It was going to be difficult to find out if the captive village women and girls were alive in the depths of those caves. He thought the creatures clever for picking such a location. It was far from the traffic of the river and the villages lining it, and it was more defendable than any bunker he could've designed.

If it hadn't been for Gabriel, they wouldn't have thought to return to these haunting digs. They'd captured that shifty Portuguese when Vandusen left him stranded on the runway after the attack. Vandusen had double-crossed him, so they'd benefited from the fact there was no honor among thieves. Gabriel was bitter. Vandusen had escaped with several of the creatures but minus him. François figured these half-human and half-chimpanzee hybrids would bring a pretty penny or franc. He couldn't be sure what Vandusen's intentions were, but he knew they'd be dark and sinister.

At first Gabriel helped in their search for the creatures, and they'd learned much. He knew those creatures well. From everything they'd managed to get out of him, these caves were special to the creatures. He told them that he'd actually been inside those dark caverns. According to Gabriel, the caves were composed of an intricate web of catacombs. On Vandusen's orders, he and his men had raided the caves and killed several of the creatures before managing to capture some. But little by little, Gabriel had grown intractable and sullen, and they couldn't get more out of him. Then one evening, he escaped, leading them on a wild goose chase across the jungles of the Congo.

There was no telling where the captives would be, if they were even still alive. François dreaded to think what those girls and women were going through. It'd been months since the creatures had raided the village next to the river, taking only the females and slaughtering all the males they could chase down. The grim scene of the aftermath still kept him awake at night. But worse, the thought of what those hideous creatures were doing to their captives chilled him to his core.

He dreaded the prospect of leading his men into those dark holes, but a plan was turning in his mind. From all they'd learned from Gabriel, the most important intelligence was that there existed an escape exit, and it was through that exit he believed the creatures had escaped with their captives during Gabriel's last raid.

François realized his lieutenant was still looking at him, waiting for further orders. "I'm thinking we could make a frontal attack at the mouth of the caves and trick them into escaping out the upper exit that shifty Portuguese told us about. We could be waiting with a squad to ambush them when they come out and hopefully rescue the native women."

The lieutenant nodded and surveyed the slopes above the caves with his field glasses.

"Take some men up the back side of the mountain and see if they can find the exit Gabriel told us about," François ordered.

The young man nodded and busied himself gathering men, but before he left, François cautioned, "Quiet as mice, mind you. They've probably set watches around all the openings. They're very clever."

***

François held up his flare gun and waited until the last of his men got into place. A light breeze waved the grasses, making it hard to see across the field, but he was sure all the creatures had gone into the cave. He watched as the last of his men cleared the rocky outcrop that marked the rear exit. It wouldn't be long now. This lieutenant was a good man. He'd proven himself by defending their compound when Vandusen had attacked them.

When the last of his men had disappeared behind the rocks, François fired the flare with a crack that echoed off the mountains.

His men charged the front of the caves while the lieutenant

held his men at the rear. François could hardly contain himself as he watched the first of his men dissolve into the shadows of the largest cave opening. The first shots startled him and the men he had waiting in reserve. "Be ready, men!" he yelled in a strained voice.

The men gripped their weapons. They'd seen the creatures work and were afraid. Some looked at each other, expressions frozen. François wondered if they'd follow him if the rest of the men needed reinforcements. *Only time will tell,* he thought. He thought many things.

He knew his plan was working when he heard shots at the rear of the caves. The shots grew from a few ragged bursts to the steady stream of automatic fire. François figured the creatures were falling for his trap. If the lieutenant and his men held their nerve, they would be able to rescue the native women, if there were any still alive. The gunfire stayed steady from both sides of the attack, front and rear. Blue smoke drifted across the valley, making it hard to see the action.

After what seemed like an eternity for François, the gunfire ceased, and the jungle sounds returned to this distant valley. He signaled his men to follow him across the clearing to help mop up. The damp grass slushed to the tread of their boots. No one spoke as they neared the outcrops. He heard the click of several safeties being disengaged. They hiked in formation, fanning the area as they neared the rear entrance.

François heard whispers from the front of their ranks, the ranks nearing the entrance. A cluster of men grew ahead of him. He froze when he reached where the men had gathered. Five women lay at their feet, whimpering, tattered, and worn. They were so weak they could barely lift their heads. Their hair was matted, and their bodies bruised and broken. Blood caked them and they reeked of foul putrefaction. The men were afraid to approach, but the real horror was their swollen bellies. All realized that they carried the unthinkable in their wombs. Several of the men raised their weapons to end this horror.

François had just enough time to step forward. "As you were, men. Secure your weapons and prepare stretchers for the wounded and these unfortunates."

The women screamed when the men neared them, covering their eyes with spread fingers. The soldiers looked back at François, confused.

"Give these poor women water—in small sips, mind you."

One of the men kneeled away from the ranks and vomited, which set several more to join him. In all his years of witnessing the atrocities of war, this was François's darkest moment. He wasn't sure how he would relay this horror of horrors to his comrades-in-arms back in the States.

Chapter Eight

A musty smell assaulted Ken as he negotiated the narrow metal stairs that led to the basement of the university library. His footsteps made a hollow sound, disturbing the quiet of the place. Why were archive sections of libraries always in basements? He smiled, realizing he could be blindfolded and would still know where he was, just by the smell.

He was meeting the head reference librarian, Tamara Dresden, and had decided to come alone, wanting to keep the peace between Consuelo and Mark. He remembered, with some amusement, the tension her appearance had caused when she'd arrived at the ranch to help them make sense of the photographs Bobby Waiter had found in Mexico. It felt like ages ago, though it hadn't been that long.

He paused and read a sign directing him to push the gate button only once, admonishing all to be patient as someone would be there directly. He noticed the door and wall were made of the same steel material he used on his transfer cages for the chimps. He carefully stuck his finger through one of the diamond-shaped openings to see if it was sharp. He'd directed his grad students to file every single diamond edge on the first cages they'd built after one of the chimps had cut its finger severely.

Light footsteps jarred him from his thoughts. He looked up and could just make out Tamara making her way down a narrow, dimly lit aisle separated by shelves of reference books, bound periodicals, and stacks of newspapers.

"Ah, Dr. Turner," she said as she unlatched the gate. "Please follow me."

Ken's eyes had trouble adjusting to the dimly lit passage as he followed her through what seemed like a maze that wound through books stacked to the ceiling. He wondered how anyone could find anything in such poor lighting. It was like entering the shafts of some underground catacombs. Deeper into the stacks, as the grad students referred to them, the musty smell grew to a stuffiness.

"It's not much farther now, Professor."

"I'm glad I have you as a guide, Tamara. I could easily get lost down here."

She smiled, looking over her shoulder, and said, "I love it down here. This is my sanctuary. I could easily live down here. It's thrilling to uncover the secrets hidden in all these old treasures."

"I'd get claustrophobic not ever seeing the light of day in this . . . this dungeon."

Ignoring his comments, Tamara said, "There's actually been a lot written about Bigfoot or Sasquatch in the Northwest. I've collected and made a list of all the sightings reported over the last two hundred years."

"Two hundred years?"

"Yes." She busied herself clearing off a space for Ken on a small couch, then motioned for him to be seated. "Actually, there's a lot of information about Bigfoot." She paused, picked up a yellow-lined notebook, and handed it to Ken. "I made a list for you of what I consider credible sightings. It's really very interesting. On the first sheet, I've listed those in the Pacific

Northwest. Many are near Willow Creek."

Ken winced at the mention of Willow Creek.

Tamara smiled. "Your secret's safe with me. I had a conversation with Fred . . . ah . . . Dr. Savage last evening. He filled me in on why you're so interested in Bigfoot and the area near that little logging town." She picked a T-shirt off the floor and handed it to Ken. "Could you please return this to Dr. Savage?"

Ken took it while looking down at the notebook to avoid her eyes. He leafed through the pages. "There seem to be a lot of sightings along Bluff Creek, which appears to be not too far from the town of Willow Creek."

Tamara nodded and inserted a cassette into a recorder. "You need to watch this. It's probably the only credible footage of a sighting to date. It was filmed in October 1967, by Roger Patterson and his colleague, Robert Gimli, in the Bluff Creek area. I had it copied this morning from some stock footage we have here. It's amazing, even though it's a copy of a copy of a copy, at least."

Ken paced the tight, little cubicle, looking at his watch as Tamara rewound the tape. He knew they were close to cuing it when he heard the high-pitched whirl of the spinning tape. He leaned over Tamara's shoulder as she pushed the play button with a loud clunk. At first the images were unsteady as the camera jerked from the ground to the sky, but finally it settled for several frames that captured a large, hairy creature walking bipedally, arms swinging, and what appeared to be breasts bouncing in unison with its stride. The creature seemed to glide effortlessly through the trees until it paused and swung around, looking back toward the camera.

Ken was stunned and amazed at how similar its locomotion and appearance were to those of the creatures they'd discovered in Africa. His voice trembled as he asked, "Could you please play it again?" They watched in silence as Tamara replayed the tape several times.

Eventually, after poring through the other resources Tamara had gathered for him, Ken moaned and stood, arching his back. "I've no idea what time it is."

"Isn't it wonderful?" Tamara nodded and looked at her watch. "It's two in the morning, Professor."

"You're kidding! It's easy to lose track of time down here. I'd need windows." Ken raised his arms and bumped an overhead fire-sprinkler pipe. "Ow!"

Tamara smiled and began stacking the books and files they had spread over her desk. "It's true, but we got a lot done—no distractions. A little different from 'working' at Frank's, I guess."

Ignoring her dig, Ken began stuffing several files and reference books into his backpack. "Which frame did you say is the best?"

"Frame 352 is thought to be the best, at least from what I've read." Tamara got up from her chair. "I'll make a copy for you when Fred comes—"

"When Dr. Savage drops by, perfect. We've covered a lot of information this evening. I believe you mentioned you have some recent newspaper articles as well?"

Tamara pulled out a manila folder and handed Ken several clippings. "These should interest you. They're stories about some recent sightings, but more importantly, the massacre of several local families in a campground just outside Willow Creek. It's horrible. The corpses of the men and women were found mutilated, and the teenage girls were gone—missing, apparently abducted. There's wild speculation surrounding this."

Ken nodded in silence as he sorted through the clippings and settled on one with a close-up shot of a large footprint.

His hands trembled as he read it. "This one is more graphic than the one Fred, ah, Dr. Savage brought me the other day at Frank's. It mentions several dismembered corpses that some ranger stumbled onto while making his rounds in the forest." Ken paused. Images of what he'd seen in Africa revisited him: the devastated villages, the corpses littering the bloodstained earth, and the dead and dying. He couldn't shake himself from this line of thought. His blood turned cold at the memory of Gordon Child being strained through the bars by Oliver, his screams drowning out the din of all the other creatures. He felt like the room had grown stuffy and hot. *I've seen this all before*, he thought, feeling light-headed. He wasn't sure if it was from remembering this nightmare, or the effects of the long evening without food or drink. He swayed and reached out for something to keep from falling.

"Are you all right, Dr. Turner?" Tamara asked, grabbing his arm to steady him. Concerned he might faint, she shook his arm and shouted, "Dr. Turner!"

"Yes. Yes, I'm okay now. I think I just need to have something to drink."

She lifted a bottle of Grant's out of a file cabinet drawer and filled two coffee mugs. Her hand trembled as she handed Ken one. It was obvious to Ken that she was beginning to wonder what she was getting herself into. But Fred could be quite persuasive.

Chapter Nine

Bobby swore as he weaved through the tangle of afternoon LA traffic, trying to dodge vehicles as he squinted at an address Hunt had scribbled on a scrap of crumpled paper. Though steering with one hand and flipping through a *Thomas Guide* with the other, he managed to keep his Volkswagen Bug in his lane on North Highland Boulevard.

After several passes and erratic U-turns, Bobby finally spied Hunt standing in front of the Gay Community Services Center across the street. "Shit!" Bobby exclaimed as he made another U-turn, setting off a symphony of blasting horns. He slowed and double-parked off the curb where Hunt stood head down, intent on reading a paper he held in his trembling hand.

Bobby honked and yelled, "Earth to Hunt!" He had to honk several times before Hunt finally looked up. Even at a distance, he could see tears streaking down Hunt's cheeks. Bobby leaned across the seat to open the passenger door since the outside handle was missing.

"Why don't you get a decent car? For Chrissakes, you have the money for it," Hunt said as he slid in, wiping his cheeks with the back of his hand.

"I like this one. My dad left it to me. Besides, he had the

seat and pedals adjusted for a midget like me. I fit and can reach everything."

Hunt still held the paper in one hand. With the other, he pulled out a handkerchief.

"What's wrong?" Bobby asked as he pulled out into traffic.

Hunt rubbed a purple blotch on his neck. "Have you ever heard of Kaposi's sarcoma lesions?"

"What?"

"I've got more than the flu, Bobby."

"Are you okay? Do you still want to meet Dr. Raven over at Canter's? Fred and Ken are back in town and have news," Bobby whispered.

"Yeah, I feel a little better now. Don't know why, but I'm actually hungry for the first time in a week. I could use some of their matzo ball soup. My Jewish friends say it will cure anything."

"So what are they saying you have?"

"The doctor's not sure what to call it. One of the nurses said they're calling it 'gay cancer' up in San Francisco."

"Fuck."

"Yeah, double fuck. That's probably how I got it in the first place."

Bobby knew if he said anything else, he'd break down, so he acted as if he had to concentrate on driving.

Hunt watched his friend for a moment before looking away. He didn't speak for the same reason.

"Don't these people watch where the hell they're going?" Bobby honked his horn at an old man and flipped him off.

Hunt laughed, shaking his head, and said, "It's more like you don't watch where you're driving this piece of shit."

Bobby smiled. "It's nice to see you're getting your sense of humor back."

Hunt spoke as he looked out the open window. "You know

how I used to tell you when I got back from the bathhouses that I had got the works?"

"Yeah." Fairfax was busy with the noon rush, so Bobby slowed down.

"Well, I did. I got the works."

"So what do we do now?" Bobby looked over at Hunt.

Hunt grabbed the steering wheel while pumping his foot on the floorboard. Bobby swerved, just missing a left-turning Mercedes.

"Christ! Your driving will probably kill me before this gay cancer."

"Sorry, I'll ask again. What are we going to do? If it's money you need, I got plenty."

"Money can't buy my way out of this crap, but thanks just the same. I'm just going to keep on living."

Bobby reached over and took Hunt's hand. Hunt jerked it away. "Keep your hands and eyes on the road. I swear you're trying to kill us!" They both laughed.

Chapter Ten

Bobby always could tell when he was entering the Jewish neighborhood in West Hollywood. No matter from which direction you came, you began seeing more shop signs in Yiddish. As he crept along in the stop-and-go traffic, he was surprised to see how crowded the sidewalks were for a weekday, and these sidewalks looked different from the rest of Hollywood. The presence of Jewish tradition was everywhere. Men of various ages wore skull caps, *kippahs*, while others sported sidelocks or *payots*. Many of the women wore modest dresses with their heads covered. Bobby smiled, thinking how much it looked like they were extras in costume on their lunch break.

Canter's, located on Fairfax Avenue, was located in the heart of the Jewish commercial district, conveniently near CBS studios—that is, convenient for anyone working in the entertainment industry. The place had hardly changed since the fifties when Bobby's parents first brought him here. His parents had loved the place, and every time he came for lunch or a late evening meal, a wave of nostalgia swept over him. He missed his parents. Show business had filled the void after losing them. He looked over at Hunt and sighed. Besides Lester, and Girlie of course, Hunt was the closest he had to family.

It hadn't taken him very long to figure out that Canter's was the perfect place to do business. Long ago he'd accidentally bumped into a producer he'd been trying to meet. The meeting had gone well in the congenial setting of "doing lunch." He realized that there was a good chance of running into almost anyone you'd been trying to arrange a meeting with by just hanging out there. The place was like a magnet for the who's who of Hollywood. If you stayed long enough—especially late in the evening or early morning—sooner or later, they'd show up.

Though established in 1931, the show business people hadn't really discovered Canter's until later in the fifties. To see that, you had only to look at the autographed pictures that covered the walls. Stepping through the front doors of this restaurant-deli was like traveling back in time. You couldn't help but notice that you stood in one of the best Jewish bakeries on the West Coast. Glass display cases filled with tempting delicacies lined the walls on both sides. Bobby paused, his mouth watering, to admire some freshly baked macaroons, his favorite. Right at eye-level, at least for Bobby, was a large tray displaying rows of them, golden brown and beckoning.

Hunt tapped Bobby on the shoulder. "I've changed my mind. Let's forget lunch and head for the lounge."

Bobby sighed, pulling himself away from the counter without ordering, and followed Hunt into the Kibitz Room adjacent to the main dining area. His eyes had trouble adjusting as they entered the lounge, a long narrow room with no windows. It was early still, so only a few patrons perched on stools at the other end, talking to the bartender. Bobby was tempted to get drunk by the well-appointed bar, but it was early, even for him.

He smiled, remembering what a Jewish friend had told him *kibitz* meant. *What was it? Gossip—exchanging unwelcome advice, or something like that.* He realized Hunt was looking at him and had the feeling they were about to *kibitz. What do you say to one of your best friends who has just found out that he may be dying of something they don't even have a proper goddamn name for?*

Hunt leaned against the bar and tried to make eye contact with the bartender. "Sorry," he said, his voice quivering. "I need a drink before I try to eat something."

Bobby nodded without saying a word and hopped onto a stool covered with plush but cracked Naugahyde. Since his legs didn't reach the floor, he tried to get comfortable by shifting his weight and pulling himself across the counter.

Hunt waited for Bobby to settle before he handed him the paper he'd been holding since he got into the car. "Take a look at this."

Bobby turned it over and began to read. He didn't notice when the bartender slid his usual Scotch on the rocks over to him.

When the bartender turned to Hunt with his usual drink, Hunt waved him off and said, "I want something different today. Something special. Can you make me one of your decadent cocktails?"

"You bet, Hunt. Are we celebrating something?"

"You might say so. Let's just say I'm getting close to a wrap."

"I didn't know you'd been working on anything lately."

"Yep, it's been an interesting project but just not long enough."

"What's the title?"

"I only have a working title right now. I'm calling it *Unfinished*. How about that drink now? Surprise me with something." Hunt winked at Bobby.

The bartender looked at both of them for a moment, but realized he was getting everything he was going to get out of either of them just now. He'd have to make them something much stronger to find out anything else.

"I swear you love drama. *Unfinished?* Really, Hunt?"

Hunt pointed at the paper. "Just keep reading my death sentence, will you?"

Bobby had trouble making sense of the medical terms, but he still caught the gist of the doctor's report, and it wasn't good. Before he could speak, the bartender returned and set a vodka martini with a sidecar in front of Hunt.

"Now we're talking," Hunt said as he took a long, slow draw.

Bobby waited while Hunt drained the glass and pulled the carafe out of the iced sidecar for a refill. Finally, when Hunt had downed the second martini and motioned for another, Bobby handed the report back and said, "So what are your options?"

Hunt waved the report as if fanning himself. "You read it. I have none. They don't even know how you get this . . . this gay cancer—or even how to treat it. I'm fucked, Bobby. I'm really fucked." He wadded up the paper and stuffed it in his pocket.

"So what are we going to do?" Bobby asked before he took a drink.

"*We* aren't going to do anything. I'm just going to keep performing. You know—the show must go on or some other silly-ass horseshit, as Lester would say."

"I wish he was here right now," Bobby said.

"Me too, but we have someone else here right now."

They watched Dr. Chris Raven walk toward them.

"Not a word about this, Bobby," Hunt said, squeezing Bobby's arm.

Bobby pried each of Hunt's fingers loose. "All right, already. That hurts!"

"What's going on with you guys? Are we having a spat?" Chris said as he motioned them over to a table. "I think a table will be more comfortable and will give us more privacy."

"You're the boss," Bobby said.

Chris looked at both of them for a moment, then whispered, "So what's going on?"

Hunt and Bobby stared at each other without saying a word.

"Come on. What's up?" Chris asked again.

Bobby broke the silence first. "Hunt's just found out he's got gay cancer."

Hunt punched Bobby in the arm. "So much for not telling anyone."

"Chris isn't just anyone." Bobby paused before whispering, "Think of Africa." They both knew if it hadn't been for Chris, they would've never gotten in or out of Africa. He ran the Wild Animal Training Center, the biggest wild animal-training business in Hollywood, and they'd used his cover of providing animals for a movie to smuggle animals and people in and out of the continent. His contacts, especially GuGu and Omar, had probably saved their lives.

"I just read an article about it in the *Times*. How long do they say you have?" Chris asked, his eyes tearing up.

"That's just it. No one knows for sure. Some live a long time and others die in months, days even, according to the doc." Hunt took a gulp that emptied his glass. He rattled the ice and waved at the bartender.

Chris frowned. "Should you be drinking?"

"It doesn't much matter now." Hunt continued to wave in the bartender's direction. "I hate poor service from surly bartenders."

Bobby yelled, "Hey, we're dry over here!"

The bartender pulled himself away from his conversation with two co-eds at the other end of the bar and ambled at his own pace toward their table, wiping the counter along the way. Hunt ordered another round.

"I still don't understand why you guys keep coming to this

dive," Chris said. "It's a poor excuse for a bar, if you ask me. It has the slowest service and the most ill-tempered servers in LA."

Bobby smiled at Hunt. "We like the atmosphere, don't we?"

Hunt ignored Bobby's comment and said, "Let's get down to business."

Chris frowned at him. "That's fine with me, but I'm not leaving until you tell me more about what's wrong with you, what this gay—"

Hunt interrupted. "It looks like Ken and Fred want to head up to the Pacific Northwest."

"Yeah, I know. It makes sense, if you think about it," Chris said.

Bobby frowned. "How so?"

"It's where the action is," Ken replied as he and Fred joined them at the table.

Bobby looked up and grinned. "So the prodigal sons return to Lotus Land!"

The bartender sighed, knowing that table wouldn't be leaving anytime soon. He gathered some menus and headed over to their table.

After greetings and orders of appetizers and drinks, Hunt asked, "What action are you talking about?"

Ken just said, "It's good to see you guys." He dropped a thick envelope in the middle of the table. "A young colleague of mine collected all this information for us. I think you'll find it very interesting, and from it I believe we can say, all roads lead to the Pacific Northwest. So get ready. We'll be searching for Bigfoot."

"Bigfoot? Great, maybe we can get the *National Enquirer* to fund our expedition. Have you lost your senses?" Bobby snatched the envelope before anyone could pick it up, then opened it and handed out the contents in silence.

They took their time reading and rereading articles and

clippings. After the bartender served another round, Ken broke the silence, saying, "What do you think?"

"Who put all this information together?" Bobby asked.

"Do you remember that friend of Mark's who helped us with the information you sent us from Mexico?"

"Yes, a pretty girl. Wasn't she Mark's girlfriend?" Hunt asked.

Ken laughed. "If I were you, I wouldn't say that if Consuelo was around."

Fred said, "Actually, Tamara is very sweet and smart, not to mention beautiful."

Ken shook his head. "Whatever, Fred—the dedicated professor as usual. What's important is that she's an excellent researcher and has really put me onto something."

"Bigfoot?" Bobby asked again.

"Yes, searching for Bigfoot is the perfect cover in Bigfoot country." Ken unfolded a newspaper clipping and handed Bobby the article about the massacre near Willow Creek and the mysterious abduction of several girls.

Hunt and Chris read the article after Bobby. No one spoke, each in their own thoughts.

"Well, what do you think?" Ken asked.

Fred finally broke the silence. "I can say one thing. This is way too familiar. It reminds me of what we found in those villages along the Congo River."

Bobby began to speak but waited for a waitress, who'd just come on shift and started clearing their table. He looked around the bar as though for the first time. "It's getting too busy in here." He smiled at Ken and continued, "I like Frank's better. Anyway, where were we? Oh yeah, I think we have some creatures on the loose."

"Exactly," Ken said. "If we find out what happened to those families, I think we'll find the creatures that Vandusen spirited off with. My thinking is he let some or all of them get away, and the only way we'll get to the bottom of this mystery is to go where the action is."

"Let's go, then!" Bobby yelled, drawing attention to their table.

"We might try going with a little less flair, Bobby." Fred looked around, surprised that the bar had filled up.

They all chuckled.

"Let's continue this meeting tomorrow at my place," Chris said. "Ten in the morning okay?"

They all nodded.

"Can I have that?" Chris asked Ken, gesturing to the envelope containing the information.

"Sure. It warrants closer inspection." Ken pushed the papers back into the envelope while everyone stood to leave.

Chris took hold of Hunt's arm. "Not so fast, my friend. We need to talk about that other thing."

Ken paused and watched Hunt and Chris head for the adjacent restaurant. He heard Hunt whisper, "I'm finally hungry, for what it's worth."

Chapter Eleven

Chris looked up from exercising a tiger to see Fred park his Grand Wagoneer next to the big cat arena. Hunt, Ken, Fred, and Bobby piled out as a cloud of dust settled around them. Chris almost lost his footing when the tiger pulled against his lead, "fixing" on Bobby. It never ceased to fascinate Chris how big cats always seemed to pick out the smallest person in a group as prey.

Ridge Kamper, the backup trainer, jumped in front of the tiger, waving a cane. "Tara, leave it!"

Bobby leaped behind the car and yelled, "I'm sure glad there's wire between us!" He looked up and down the arena fencing. "Are you sure this wire is secure?"

Fred and the others walked over to Chris, ignoring Bobby. "Nice-looking tiger, Chris," he said. "Is it a Bengal?"

"The best working one in the business. Right, Ridge?" Chris replied as he helped Ridge readjust the chain collar around the tiger's neck. Ridge was one of the best big cat trainers in the business and had worked for WATC for several years. Chris was good at attracting the best talent in Hollywood.

Ridge smiled and waved at Bobby as he released the tiger to run free inside the arena. The tiger made a beeline directly toward Bobby, stopping short just before he hit the wire that separated them.

"Hell, I'm out of here. Ridge, you're an asshole." Bobby tugged on Hunt's arm, then beckoned him to follow as he retreated across the lawn to the open French doors of the clubhouse. Ken and Fred ambled after them. Once inside, Bobby shut both doors, clicked the door lock, and shook the doors to test it. The men all chuckled.

Chris yelled from outside, "Let me wrap this up with Ridge and I'll be right in." He grinned and added, "I'll test this wire. Looks like some of it's coming loose." He laughed as he walked away.

"Very funny!" Bobby shouted from inside.

A short while later, Chris knocked on the French doors that Bobby had locked and waited for Fred to let him in. "Thanks," Chris said as he entered with Ridge. He paused to let his eyes adjust to the dim light in the clubhouse's grand room.

A fire in the stone fireplace and the heat lamps of several reptile cages provided the only light. Bobby and Hunt stood with their backs against the heat of the crackling log fire. Chris smiled at the contrast between them. Hunt was close to six feet tall and Bobby was half that. In fact, Bobby could've walked right into the hearth without ducking his head.

The WATC had been a hunting lodge for the rich and famous before Chris bought and converted it. Some of the areas remained unchanged, and he'd repurposed others. The skeet tower had been converted to a rehab and release center for injured raptors, but the clubhouse still had a flock of stuffed geese hanging in formation from the high-raftered ceiling. Some of the old photos of celebrities who'd been hunting guests, like John Wayne and Bill Holden, still hung on the walls, but several reptile cages lined the walls. This grand room was where

Chris held meetings and taught classes on animal training and behavior.

He motioned everyone to take a seat on the hodgepodge of couches and stuffed chairs that appointed the room, then stood in front of the fireplace on a thick bearskin rug. When he leaned over to whisper something to Ken, his tall, lanky frame cast a shadow that the crackling fire made dance off the walls.

"Can we have a little light on the subject?" Bobby asked as he watched a large Burmese python nosing the glass of its cage. "This place gives me the creeps!"

"Sure, Bobby." Chris smiled and motioned Ridge to flip on some overhead lights. He ran his fingers through his thick, dark hair and smiled before continuing, "I just thought, dark rooms for dark deeds."

Everyone laughed nervously. Fred broke the mood by saying, "Let's get this meeting going so we can all have something to drink and eat."

Chris nodded to Ridge. "Best get the BBQ going before our guests have a food riot."

Ridge smiled. "Emu or kangaroo?"

"Both," Chris answered but held his hand up to stop Ridge at the door, "Except for Bobby. Fillet some python for him."

The room filled with laughter and light before Bobby could say anything.

Chris waited for the laughter to die down, cleared his throat, and lowered his voice to just above a whisper. "It's been just over a year since we made it back from our adventures." He watched as each of his friends let that settle before continuing. "Each of us has tried to return to some kind of normalcy. Some of us have been able to do that better than others. I, for one, have wondered why none of us have bumped into Vandusen or one of his thugs." Everyone nodded. "It's been a real mystery what happened after we lost their trail in Rotterdam. They got on that cargo ship and seemed to disappear." Chris paused and let that set in before stretching his tall, lanky body and continuing, "Well, I think the mystery is settled with all this latest news from up north in Willow Creek."

Ken interrupted. "We can't be absolutely sure this incident has anything to do with the hybrid creatures."

"Wouldn't you like to know for sure?" Chris asked. He wiped his forehead with a red bandanna he always kept in his faded jeans.

"Of course," Ken replied. "We want to make sure we're not responsible, and either way, we should do what we can to put a stop to all of this, and at the same time, study and protect what's out there."

"That's a big order. How do you plan to do that?" Chris asked.

"We'll head up and investigate and see what we can find out. After that, who knows?" Ken said, looking at the others.

Chris smiled. "Sounds like a good plan to me. How can I help?"

Fred jumped in, saying, "We could use some of your transfer cages and a trailer. And maybe a little help from Dusty and Lester."

"You got it."

"Somebody mentioned my name?" Dusty said as he slipped in through the back door.

"Are you up to teaming up with Lester and moving Oliver and Danny?" Chris asked.

Dusty shrugged. "Sure. Where?"

"Not sure yet," Ken said.

"Just you and Lester will be up in Reno to help Mary and the crew, since Fred and Ken will be gone," Chris said.

Ken stood, wandered over to the fire, and pitched in a log. "I got a feeling some of Vandusen's men are going to show up, now that everything has gone to shit up north. I think we're going to get paid a visit by some of those thugs from the DOD or wherever those assholes come from."

"Great!" Bobby said, looking out the window.

Ignoring Bobby, Ken continued, "We just need to be proactive this time. They started all this. We need to finish it, once and for all."

Chris nodded. "All right, so it's settled, then. Ken, Bobby, Hunt, and Fred will head up to—where was it?—Willow Creek? Ken can pick up Mark in Reno. Lester and Dusty can fill in the gap that'll leave and head up to Reno to keep an eye on things there."

Ken looked at Dusty. "You and Lester need to be ready to move Danny and Oliver if you get the word from us."

"Where and when are you planning on moving them?" Dusty asked.

"The 'when' could be when we've found a better home for them or to keep them out of Vandusen's hands. The 'where' is still up in the air. Just be ready."

Dusty nodded.

The group sat in silence, listening to the crackling fire. Ridge broke the mood when he swung open the double doors, letting the BBQ aroma drift in.

Bobby jumped up, looked at Chris, and said, "Well, I'm not going to be at the end of the line behind His Majesty over here like last time. Let's forget this for a while and fill our guts."

They followed Bobby outside to the BBQ pits on the lawn just as the sun set behind the trees that lined the Santa Ana river.

Ken motioned Fred toward him and whispered, "For all his complaining, Bobby has the heart of a lion." They both laughed and lined up at the end of the chow line with Chris.

Chapter Twelve

Five months earlier

The creatures stumbled over the boulders that skirted the river, in search of a shallow spot to cross. The river ran swift and felt cold, but they needed to reach the other side and continue the search for the rest of their troop. Though the humans surely had them hidden, they felt they were near. They could sense it. The forest was new territory for them, and they were lost. The roar of the river competed with the rest of the forest sounds.

Almost one cycle of the moon had passed since they'd wakened to find themselves lying in the wreckage of the strange machine that had taken them up into the night sky like a bird. After recovering, they'd carried off their dead and injured to the lava caves they'd found nearby. Ever since, they'd been searching for the rest of their kindred—the ones the humans still held captive—and they wouldn't stop their search until they found them.

The leader paused and looked around, unsure of his surroundings—a strange land covered with trees, cold and rocky, so different from the jungles of his homeland. Fortunately, there were places to live and hide in, like the caves they'd found. One of the females had led him to it after she'd found it while gathering berries. The berries were sweet and plentiful. They darkened their lips after gorging. He sighed. They could make this work, but not until their troop was whole again.

He looked up, startled by the wind that howled in a blast high up in the treetops. These trees were so different from the jungle. Tall and sparse, they smelled fresh but pungent. He sniffed the air. Cold and fresh. Absent of rot. His eyes followed the creamy, billowing clouds as they raced overhead, ripping apart on the distant peaks that accentuated the bright azure sky. This was wild country. They'd have to settle into it with caution.

Besides the humans, other creatures lurked in these wilds— many of them and all different from what he knew—and some were dangerous. A giant beast who walked on four legs but rose onto its hind legs when angry had killed one of their clan. It had sharp claws and teeth, and beady eyes. He'd spied on the humans trapping one for fur. Another of his troop had stumbled onto one of those traps and died from the injuries. Their numbers were dwindling. Even though they were cold and hungry, they had to be careful. He wished Oliver and Danny were with them. They would know what to do. They were their real leaders, as proven by the markings—two over the six.

Other creatures, more like them but not human, also lived here. They'd spied them at a distance, walking on twos as they did, filing along a ridge. They'd followed those creatures' tracks since dawn but lost them on the rocky shore of the river. The leader welcomed the warmth of the sun as they stood in the clearing, but he didn't like how exposed they were to the eyes of the forest. He felt they were being watched.

One of the creatures raced back toward them. All hunkered down, darting furtive glances about, their hair bristling. "Come, follow," he signed.

The troop hesitated, looking at their leader.

He stared in the direction from which the creature had come but saw nothing.

Realizing the rest of his clan were watching him, he signed, "Go, now." He couldn't let them know he felt unsure, afraid even. Some wanted to take his place.

He signaled them to move forward, and they picked their way through the boulders, following the creature who'd urged them to follow him. The walls of the river valley closed in around them when they reached a sharp bend where they had to climb over a tangle of logs. He froze when he reached the other side and saw a large wooden structure that spanned the river. Humans made this. It smelled of them. The troop ran ahead to the edge of it but wouldn't cross it. One creature touched the wood and withdrew his hand as though it burned him. But the leader knew it was most likely fear that made him pull away. The rest hooted, filling the narrow canyon with their cries.

"Quiet. Follow," the leader signed. He took a tentative step onto the structure, hesitated when it creaked under his weight, and looked down toward the rushing river below. The planks under his feet swayed, and he reached for a frayed rope above to steady himself. He looked back and saw his whole troop bunched together, afraid to follow, but he had to cross the river. He had to be a leader. Clouds of mist rose up around him, dampening his hair and fogging his view to the other side. Cold drops trickled down his face, but his arm was too damp to wipe it dry. If he wanted to stay the leader, he had no choice but to step forward and cross. He caught the scent of something putrid carried by the breeze—something foul or dead in the trees at the other end in the shadows—and glared back at the troop, still vacillating. He snarled, showing his teeth, and signed, "Come now. Hurry."

Several of the troop gingerly stepped onto the planks, making it bounce. Some raced back onto the bank, but the leader paid them no heed and continued across. His mind was made up. Gusts of wind made the structure sway. The creatures froze, looking from side to side, and that's when they spied the other creatures—like them but not them. They'd been watching them from the bank below.

At first, the leader took them to be their lost companions—until they moved into the sunlight on the rocky shoreline. Though not human, they weren't like them either. They walked on twos but stood a head taller than the tallest of the leader's clan. They had cinnamon-colored hair, long and matted. The wind carried their stench across the river—a smell so foul and rotten that it made the leader retch. He realized that some were racing to cut them off at the other side, while the rest tried to wade across the swift current to block their retreat. They'd been lurking in the shadows of the woods, waiting for them. The leader didn't have much time. His clan was vulnerable. Their best chance was to retreat back the way they'd come before any of the others made it across the river.

Suddenly, screams wailed above the roaring river. The leader and his troop froze, watching as the current swept several of the ambushers away. The leader raced back across the bridge, pushed his way through his troop and scrambled down the steep bank to the edge of the river. Several of his group followed him, and they watched as the racing current swallowed several of the ambushers. Without thinking, he reached for rope that hung from the structure, jerked it repeatedly until it snapped, then made several attempts to throw the rope in the direction of a creature hanging onto a rock. It became easier to throw once wet, and finally, it landed just within reach of the creature. The creature took hold and several of the troop hauled on the rope, heaving against the current, to slowly pull the creature to shore. It crawled from the water and collapsed at their feet. The leader kicked at the limp body with his foot, while the ambushers stood silent on the other side of the river, watching.

When the creature didn't move, the leader picked up a stick and poked it. This time it stirred. All sprang back and watched as it tried to push up to its knees. The leader stooped to help it stand and steadied it as it wobbled, trying to walk. The creature had turned from ambusher to rescued. The leader stepped back and waited. The creature looked around, as though trying to get its bearings, then turned and crossed the structure to rejoin the ambushers, paying them no heed.

Somehow, the leader knew it would be safe to follow and cross now, so he gathered his troop. The ambushers stood as if in a daze, watching the leader's clan file across the structure toward them. As he neared the group blocking his way, the leader fought the urge to charge. His hair puffed up, and he could feel rage grow in his throat. He puckered his lips, covering his teeth, as he stepped near where they'd gathered, then he stopped, his clan halting behind him.

The groups stared at each other without moving while the rescued beast limped back to its comrades. It struggled to keep standing, and some stepped forward to help steady it. The leader raised his hand, palm outward, in a sign of peace. The ambushers looked from one to another, and finally, as though understanding the signal, several signaled back in the same way. Still holding his hand palm out, the leader stepped toward them. The ambushers parted to make way for them, then turned and faded into the shadows of the trees without a sound. Each group went its separate way, ignoring each other as they disappeared into the shoulder-high ferns.

***

The creatures huddled close together, watching their leader grind grooved lines into the white limestone walls of the cave. They sat to one side, away from a puddle forming from rain that showered from an opening above them. The dying sunlight reflected off the drops, giving just enough light to see the drawings on the walls and ceiling. They'd found a sacred place in this wild land. A place where others had come before them to leave their marks, just as their leader was doing now. All were quiet and did not stir.

The leader carved two over six in a blank spot on the wall, being careful not to deface the other drawings. Most of the drawings depicted the hunt. They knew not to touch them. Other forms on the walls looked like large creatures who walked on twos like them—like the ones they'd seen at the river.

The leader finished the drawing by cutting his gnarled palm with a piece of sharp obsidian and smearing the lines until they were blood red. The troop's hoots echoed deep into the caverns. Knowing they'd staked their claim, they hooted louder. They would be the masters of this land, just as they'd been in their homeland—or would they?

The leader was unsure because of the other creatures they'd met at the river. He knew they'd meet them again, and soon. They'd been lucky at the river. In his clouded thoughts, he didn't understand why he'd rescued the one who had tried to ambush them. But he had, and that act had given them a pass, though outnumbered. He turned and signed to the troop, "Go now."

The creatures looked at each other, confused, as it was warm and dry in the cave, but the leader knew this was a place for worship, not living. This was a place for the other world of spirits. Other caves would provide homes for the living, and they'd have to search for one now in the fading light and pouring rain.

He signed again, "Hurry. Go," and gnashed his teeth.

The creatures paused at the mouth of the cave until their leader stepped out into the rain and signaled them to follow. They followed.

The leader sensed they were being followed before he heard the faint rustling in the shadows. The trail that led to their missing comrades had gone cold just like the air that hung in the valley. He hesitated at the edge of an open meadow, fearing being exposed. The troop gathered around him, looking from each other to him. Something was out there, and he didn't know what it was. This new territory was hard to read. It was cold and damp, darker than their homeland. The smells were unfamiliar, and the big creatures they had encountered at the river worried him.

He looked up at the clouds ripping over the rocky ridges that surrounded them, unsure what weather was coming. Two mornings ago, they'd woken to freezing particles falling from the sky. This was a new experience, and they didn't know how to deal with it, or more importantly, predict it. Finally, he motioned his troop to follow as he stepped into the open and made haste across the wet, spongy meadow. They had to jump over or wade through the meandering ribbons of trickling creeks that fed the tall grass. A chill passed over him as he reached the shadows of the other side of the clearing. Something had moved in the thickets.

A tall, shaggy-haired creature stepped out of the shadows and held his hand up in a gesture calling them to halt.

The leader's hair bristled, and he gnashed his teeth. He and his troop moved back and forth, hesitating, unsure if they should charge or retreat. The leader signed, "Stay," and the group crept back several strides, leaving him alone to face what might come next.

The bigfoot walked further into the open, paused in front of the leader, and held his hand up above his head with his palm facing out.

The leader returned the gesture as he looked at this strange creature. A calmness passed over him, and he saw that the rest of his troop had settled down as well. A warmth grew in them that melted their fear away. The leader felt these beings were not a threat but wanted to help them. His rage subsided.

The bigfoot stood a shoulder above the leader. His amber hair hung in thick shags which covered the features of his face. The leader looked at each of them, tilting his head from side to side. Another stepped out of the woods and held something out to the leader. He realized it was wreckage from the metal bird that had fallen out of the sky. He nodded to the bigfoots.

The bigfoot motioned the creatures to follow as they turned up a dark, narrow path that weaved through the trees and up a slope that led to a rocky ridge above.

The leader paused, looked over his shoulder, and motioned his troop to follow.

Chapter Thirteen

Highway 299 from the 101 to Willow Creek wound through the forest like a tentacle. For most of the way, it skirted the deep ravine the Trinity River cut into this wild and primitive wilderness. Spruce and other conifers closed in on the narrow two-lane ribbon, making it hard to see around the curves that often hid unwelcome surprises like logging trucks, loaded with freshly cut old growth, barreling downhill on their way to market. Ken had to squeeze over to the very edge of the road to prevent their little Hertz rental car being crushed like a beer can. He hunched over, gripping the steering wheel so tightly his hands cramped.

"Christ, those trucks are big!" He adjusted his rearview mirror and could see Fred stretched across the back seat, sleeping, his head leaning against Mark. Hunt slumped in the remaining space, his head back, mouth wide open, snoring. Bobby was sitting shotgun, being Bobby.

"How much further is it to Willow Creek?" Bobby asked.

"We've a ways to go yet. Hopefully, we'll meet Sandy in town before the parade starts. Tamara says the parade is the best time to catch up with some of the players in this Bigfoot game," Ken replied as he reached for his thermos.

"And then what?" Bobby asked.

Ken dumped coffee in his lap when he swerved, just missing another truck blowing pass them. "Christ! Let me concentrate on keeping us on the road, right now," he said.

Bobby nodded. "That was close. I guess size is might with these assholes."

Ken settled back to driving. He wished Mary was here and driving this damn road for him. He'd decided that Mary would join them later, after Lester came up to Reno to help with Oliver and Danny. At least, that was the plan, but who knew how things would turn out on this rollercoaster of an adventure?

Bobby smirked, looking back at Fred and Hunt still sleeping. He was tempted to wake them up, but he settled back to his thoughts as the road straightened out at the summit. From there, he caught glimpses of the river glimmering far below. The surrounding mountains rose around them in steep, almost vertical faces. He thought the area, the Trinity Alps, aptly named. The forest was thick and dense. Even at high noon, he couldn't see beyond the shadows of the dense undergrowth that filled in between the trees. Anything could be in there. You could brush up against a bigfoot in those shadows and never see it, if it didn't want to be seen.

***

"So what are we doing here?" Fred asked.

They stood in front of the Willow Creek Variety Store, watching as the citizens of Willow Creek scurried from shop to shop, putting the final touches on the street decorations for the weekend's festivities, Bigfoot Daze.

Bobby snapped and wound his Instamatic. "This place is Bigfoot-crazy. What a bunch of kooks!"

"Why don't you yell a little louder, Bobby?" Ken said as he pulled Bobby toward him by his belt. "I'm sure the townsfolk will appreciate what you have to say." He turned to the others. "Come over here, you guys. We need to set some ground rules for our visit."

The team, including Sandy, who'd met them in front of the store, gathered around Ken as he and Fred took a seat on a bench in front of the store.

Ken looked around before continuing, "The proprietor at this store is Al Hodgson. According to Tamara, Al was the first person Roger Patterson talked to after he observed and filmed what he claims was a female bigfoot. Patterson and his friend Robert Gimli say they saw the female bigfoot at Bluff Creek, up in the Trinity Alps. That's pretty close to here, as the crow flies, and the campground where the massacre occurred is just up the road as well." Tamara showed me several articles that make it clear that Al has an expansive collection of Bigfoot artifacts like casts of tracks, hair samples, and a lot more. Evidently, this is the guy you come to if you want to report a sighting. I saw one newspaper clipping that shows him holding a thick scrapbook of articles concerning Bigfoot. I think a good start for our little field trip would be to have a chat with Al." Ken paused, staring at Bobby. "We need to keep a low profile around here. A lot of these people are believers, and we're going to need their cooperation. Especially Al's."

"But really, Bigfoot?" Bobby whispered.

Sandy sat beside Ken and said, "Think about it, Bobby. This event is a perfect time to poke around and ask some questions. Look around. The place is crawling with tourists. We need to find out more about this new primate facility being built around here, and there's a pretty good chance Vandusen and his cronies are somehow involved. Besides, we have some of our own creatures to account for."

"But Bigfoot?" Bobby grimaced with disbelief.

"Yes, Bigfoot, if that helps us blend in and have a look around," Sandy said. "Right now, there's more outsiders than locals for the Daze, not to mention all the law enforcement still hanging around. It's the perfect time to blend in and listen and learn."

The group watched as people began lining the streets with lawn chairs and blankets. Smoke and aromas from the food stands filled the air.

Bobby scowled. "They're still going to hold this event, despite what's happened?"

Fred threw up his hands. "I suppose even here, the show must go on."

Ken motioned the group to follow him up the street and said, "Let's break up and blend into the crowd. We can meet up back here after the parade, if I don't see you before."

***

Ken made slow progress weaving through the parade crowd, amazed at how many people had turned out on this long weekend in September to take part in Bigfoot Daze. He had to hug the shops that lined the main street to avoid the surge of people picking up and leaving at the tail end of the parade. He hurried, as he wanted to find Fred and the rest of the group and see if they'd found out anything while poking around, to use Sandy's words. Their next step was to find someone who might be able to guide them into the backcountry.

Ken paused under the shade of an awning. The sun was intense for September. Through the crowd, he spotted Fred deep in conversation with a man and smiled at the odd contrast of the two men animated in their discussion sitting below a giant wooden statue of Bigfoot. The statue was carved out of what looked like a local redwood. Its head was set on huge, broad shoulders, absent a neck. Its arms reached below its knees, and it towered over them, stoic. Ken had the feeling it was staring right through him.

He assumed the man Fred sat with was a local indigenous person. His long, silky hair and turquoise and silver jewelry were a giveaway. They both stood up as Ken approached.

Fred smiled. "Here you are."

Ken took a closer look at the man standing next to Fred. Slight of frame, he stood stooped over and a head shorter than Fred. He peered at Ken with dark, piercing eyes that seemed to take in everything. His gnarled and calloused hands made it obvious the man worked with his hands.

"I was hoping to make it back to Al's store before he closes shop," Ken said to Fred as he pointed back up the street.

"No need for that now, Ken. Let me introduce Jimmy Two-Feathers." Fred nodded toward the man beside him. "Jimmy's a bit of a local celebrity around these parts. He lives nearby, on the Hupa Res, and has actually seen Bigfoot, but more importantly, he's been part of several expeditions that journeyed out into the backcountry in search of Bigfoot."

Jimmy Two-Feathers smiled and stepped forward to shake Ken's hand. "I hear you want to go up there." He jerked his thumb back over his shoulder in the direction of the distant mountains.

Ken nodded. "We'd like to see if there's any connection between Bigfoot and what happened to those families recently."

"So you believe in Ohmah?" Jimmy grinned. A gold tooth gleamed, setting off his perfect white teeth. The contrast between his dark gums, skin, and teeth made them seem even whiter.

A small leather pouch decorated with fine beadwork detailing a bigfoot looking over its shoulder hung around his neck. Jimmy pointed at the statue towering over them and said, "That's about the right size, you know."

Fred and Ken looked the statue up and down but said nothing.

Chapter Fourteen

Kelly finally reached the last hill before Willow Creek and looked back at the mountains he'd just left. He sighed and hustled down to the streets of the little village he called home.

What next?

Kelly walked toward the community center as people busied themselves cleaning the streets of the trash left from Bigfoot Daze. No one noticed him. He was tired and needed a shower and a nap, but business first. He needed to check in with the sheriff and report what he'd found.

What have I found?

Already, he was beginning to doubt what he'd seen in those mountains. It seemed like a dream, or more like a nightmare.

He paused at the glass doors of the community center and wiped the sweat-caked dirt from his face before stepping inside. He walked to the counter, shivering from the air conditioning, and rang the bell that sat on it.

The secretary looked up from her desk and smiled. "Jim!"

"Hi, Margie. Is the boss in?" he asked.

"He's in with someone. Let me see if he can break away." Before she reached the back of the room, she paused and turned back. "Are you okay?"

"Yes, I'm just tired and need to get cleaned up and go to bed." Kelly brushed his shirt off and ran his fingers through his hair to straighten it.

She nodded, knocked on the office door, and disappeared inside.

Kelly looked around the center, thinking how different it was from a few weeks ago when it was bustling with media and news reporters.

How quick people forget, he thought. But he didn't.

"He'll see you now," the secretary said, jerking him from his thoughts. She watched as he made his way to the back.

***

"Lt. Jim Kelly," the sheriff said as he stood from his desk. "There's someone I'd like you to meet. Please say hi to Lt. John Sandy of the Washoe County Sheriff's Department. He's come all the way up from Reno."

Kelly looked from the sheriff to Sandy before saying, "Nice to meet you, Lt. Sandy. What brings you to our neck of the woods?"

Sandy smiled. "I'm here on a missing—investigation."

"Who you looking for?" Kelly asked.

"A Dr. Melon. The professor went missing several months ago from the campus of the University of Nevada, Reno. We suspect foul play."

"So why here?"

"I believe you have a research facility being built just outside of town." Sandy picked his words carefully. "We think there might be a connection."

"How so?"

"The facility is being built by the Department of Defense.

It's a top secret facility, so our department is having trouble getting any information on what it does or who works there. We've received intel recently that suggests he may be working there. We'd like to confirm this information. I just wanted to check in with your department out of courtesy."

"We greatly appreciate that, Lieutenant," the sheriff said. "How can we be of assistance?"

Kelly had a feeling this big-city lieutenant wasn't telling them everything. No doubt the sheriff felt the same and would keep an eye on him.

"Any information you could give me on this new facility would be very helpful," Sandy replied. "Also, I'd like to visit there, so any support you can give me in my investigation would be most welcome."

The sheriff walked over to Kelly, put his arm around him, and said, "We have just the man who can help you. Jim's your guide. He knows this country like the back of his hand. In fact, he's just back from tracking what or who perpetrated the recent homicides near here."

"That's great news, and I'll be happy to share any information I procure in my investigation with you," Sandy said.

Kelly looked from the sheriff to Sandy. He didn't like the direction this meeting was headed, but he worked for the sheriff's department, at least on this investigation, so he'd have to cooperate. "Glad to be of service." Looking at the sheriff, he continued, "Now, I'd like to make my report." He hesitated, giving a sideways glance at Sandy.

"I think we can speak freely with the lieutenant present," the sheriff said, sitting back down behind his desk.

Sandy pulled two chairs up to the desk and motioned for Kelly to take a seat.

Kelly slumped into the chair with a moan. He paused for a

moment, trying to decide where to start. Sandy and the sheriff waited. Kelly decided his best course was to be honest and not leave anything out, even if doing so would tag him as a kook. He looked up at the ceiling and began, "There's something out there, and it's not normal."

Sandy and the sheriff glanced at each other, but Kelly continued before they could say anything. "I heard cries and whistles out there, deep in the forest, and they weren't like any animal I'd ever heard before."

The sheriff shuffled some papers on his desk and glanced out the window before saying, "You're tired, Jim. Maybe you should get some rest before you make your report." He shrugged his shoulders at Sandy.

Shifting in his chair as though trying to get comfortable, Sandy asked, "Bigfoot?"

"Why that?" the sheriff asked.

"It's just that I'm traveling with several scientists who are searching for Bigfoot. I invited them along because they know Dr. Melon—the man I'm looking for. I thought they might be helpful in getting me into that research facility."

Kelly interrupted before the sheriff could speak. "There's more. I found this." He pulled the tennis shoe out of his pack and handed it to the sheriff.

The sheriff froze at the sight of it for a moment, then turned it over and over before speaking. "I know the girl this belongs to . . .We have the other shoe in the evidence box. Where did you find it?"

Though still uncomfortable sharing these details with Sandy present, Kelly answered, "Up Bluff Creek, where the Trinity and Klamath merge."

"Christ! You were *waaay* out there," the sheriff said.

Kelly nodded without saying more.

The sheriff handed the tennis shoe to Sandy. "I can't believe anyone would carry that shoe twenty miles into the backcountry. I'm guessing whoever or whatever did this carried at least one girl up into the mountains."

"What do you plan to do?" Sandy asked.

Kelly and the sheriff looked at each other before the sheriff said, "Finding anything out in the backcountry is like hoping to find a needle in a haystack."

Kelly stood, walked to the window, and stared at the distant mountains. "A good tracker will do better than an army tramping around the woods."

The sheriff nodded in agreement. "And we have a good tracker."

"However," Kelly continued, "I can use help investigating some wreckage I found in one of the meadows."

The sheriff frowned. "What are you talking about?"

"I found what looks like the wreckage of a plane crash."

"We have no record of any missing planes or any crashes in this area."

"I know. That's what's so weird about this. It's fairly recent, and there's more." He pulled the bags of hair and blood samples out of his backpack and handed them to him. "Could you run some tests on these? The hair doesn't look like it belongs to any animal I'm familiar with, and there were broken cages in the wreckage." He frowned. Was that a glimmer of excitement he caught in the lieutenant's eyes?

The sheriff picked up the phone and called the crime lab in Eureka.

Sandy, his expression quickly schooled into one of cool professional interest, shuffled his chair and cleared his throat. "I might be able to help. The scientists I mentioned are experts in animal studies. They could be useful in helping you ID the hair samples."

The sheriff looked from Kelly to Sandy. "We can always use help. Maybe you can show us some big-city evidence techniques. In fact, why don't you take a look at this crash site?"

Before Sandy could answer, Kelly said, "I'm sure Detective Sandy has enough on his plate without stomping around the forest with me."

"Actually," Sandy said, "I'd like to take a look around, especially if it gives me an excuse to check on that new primate facility. And I don't believe in coincidences in our line of work. It seems odd that there'd be a plane crash with cages and animal hair in the same area they're building a primate facility that may be linked to Dr. Melon."

Before Kelly could respond, the sheriff said, "Well then, that's settled." He stood and looked at the door.

The meeting was over.

Kelly strode out without speaking to this Lt. Sandy character. The meeting had seemed like it would never end, and he was glad to get back outside. He'd received permission to lead a whole crime lab team up to the crash site, but he wasn't sure about working with Sandy. He liked to work alone. He could concentrate better and move faster. Why did the sheriff want them to work together?

He was tired and needed to get some sleep, so he wouldn't think about that or anything else right now. He'd think clearer after he got some rest and a good meal. He thought of going home but knew the house would be up and stirring with the daily routine of three kids and his wife. He couldn't face that just yet, and there'd be all the questions from his wife. He decided to head back to headquarters and crash in one of the cabins they kept ready for the seasonal firefighters. He'd meet Sandy later and discuss how they could cooperate. Sandy wanted information on this facility the government was building at the old logging camp near the Hupa Reservation, and Kelly had wondered about it since he'd read a report the superintendent had sent him. It seemed like a very remote location to build a primate center. But it might mean jobs for the locals, and god knows, the locals needed jobs ever since logging had dropped off because the spotted owl had been . . . spotted.

Willow Creek was getting back to normal. Jim could hardly tell the parade and other activities of Bigfoot Daze had ever happened. He'd missed it this year as he'd been tracking, but it seemed odd to see the routine of the town returning. Some media vans were parked near the hardware store, so he turned down a side street. The last thing he wanted was to talk to anyone, especially a reporter, about his recent activities. He crossed the street and disappeared into an alley.

The parking lot was full behind the Bigfoot Motel, so there were still some people in town. He'd have to be careful where he met Lt. Sandy. He pulled a business card from his shirt pocket and looked at the number scribbled on the other side. He recognized it as that of the motel. That might be the best place to meet. He changed course and walked toward the office. He figured that if he didn't get this meeting over, he wouldn't sleep anyway.

***

The motel door opened to Sandy smiling. "Come in, come in." He motioned Kelly into the cluttered room. Piles of clothes lay on the two unmade twin beds. "You'll have to excuse the mess," he said. "We had to share rooms because of Bigfoot Daze. Please sit down."

Kelly helped Sandy clear some books off a wicker chair at a desk next to a window that looked out on the parking lot, then he sat down. "I hope you don't mind me dropping in like this, but I got to thinking that it might make sense not to call too much attention to ourselves by meeting in a more public place. This is a small town, and people will talk, you know."

Sandy nodded. "Absolutely, no problem on my end. Our group would like to keep a low profile while we poke around up here."

Kelly looked around the room and settled on what look like two sets of luggage. He sensed that Sandy was nervous.

Sandy smiled and said, "You're probably wondering who 'our group' is."

"You mentioned that you're not alone up here. You have some help?"

"Yes, bigfoot researchers who were coming up here anyway for the festivities."

Kelly wondered if this was a cover, and this Lt. Sandy and his friends were somehow mixed up in the massacre and the missing girls. But he decided to play along, at least for now. "So where are they now?"

Kelly thought Sandy would be a great poker player. His face gave nothing away. Kelly hesitated before saying, "They met a local who agreed to guide them into the backcountry. A place called Bluff Creek, I believe. They're due back today, if all goes well."

"It rarely does out there. Who did they go with?" Kelly asked.

"A character who calls himself Jimmy Two-Feathers."

Kelly nodded. "I know him. He is a real character, but you could've done a lot worse. He's honest enough."

Sandy scowled. "I'm not sure I like the sound of 'honest enough.' What do you mean?"

Kelly smiled. "There's a lot of people living here who would gladly take your money and ditch you out there, or worse."

"Hopefully my friends will be back soon."

Now the man seemed nervous. Kelly couldn't tell if he was worried about his friends or trying to pick his words carefully to cover up something.

They sat without a word then, neither wanting to be the first to start a conversation, but when Kelly thought they'd reached the point of moving from awkward to rude, he asked, "So what exactly is your mission up here, Lieutenant?"

"As I said, I'm looking for a missing person. But before I go any further, could I ask what it was you thought you heard on your recent trip?"

"I'm not sure. After I saw the reaction the sheriff had—you know, about me getting some rest and all—I decided to show him this later." Kelly pulled out something wrapped in newspaper and laid it gently on the table next to them.

"With your permission?" After receiving a nod, Sandy took his time to unwrap the plaster mold of the footprint Kelly had made. He held it to the window for better light.

Kelly watched as Sandy took in every detail. "So what do you think?" Kelly asked.

"It's huge and very humanlike," Sandy said as he lowered it to compare with his foot.

"Yes." Kelly watched Sandy's expressions carefully.

Sandy handed the mold back to Kelly. "Several of the people I'm traveling with are scientists. We should show this to them."

Kelly nodded and wrapped the mold back up. "It might be illuminating to get an expert opinion."

"So is it really Bigfoot?" Sandy said, looking out the window.

Kelly shrugged. "Who can say? There is something out there, and I mean to find it."

"Let us help you." Sandy paused, noticing Kelly's furrowed brow. "We're all experienced outdoor people, and what better team members to have than some primate specialists?"

Kelly raised an eyebrow. "I thought you said they were Bigfoot scientists."

"They believe if Bigfoot exists, it's some kind of primate."

"It would be a mighty big primate."

Sandy nodded. "Let's throw in together and see what clues we can turn up. I think the missing person I'm investigating, this massacre, and that new 'secret' facility are somehow connected."

"What do you mean?"

"In my investigation, everything leads back to that facility."

Kelly realized there was a lot Sandy was not telling him. But he was tired and not thinking clearly. "I'm staying near here at the headquarters, actually, in one of the cabins, tonight. What say we meet later tonight when your friends get back? If they get back."

Sandy stood as Kelly made his exit.

The wind picked up as he made his way across the back parking lot. He smiled at the cage on display that advertised it was used to hold Bigfoot. The large cage, built of steel bars, stood a good ten feet tall. A giant could stand up in it. He shook his head. From the size of the footprint, he guessed it was just about the right size.

He saw no one else on his way to a much-needed shower and nap.

Chapter Fifteen

Evening had approached by the time Kelly awoke, feeling refreshed. His hand made several squeaks as he wiped the steam off the bathroom mirror and eyed his reflection. This business was graying him. He'd have to have his wife give him a proper trim. That usually got the gray out. But he planned to bunk in the forest service quarters for a few more days instead of going home. He liked that old, single-wide trailer at the fire camp near his official office. He could always count on getting some rest there without being bothered. Besides, it reminded him of simpler times from his misspent youth. He smiled at the memories.

After his meeting with Lt. Sandy, he'd felt drained and had needed to crash. He knew his wife and daughters were waiting to hear about his search, but he didn't want to share what he'd turned up, not yet. This whole case unnerved him. He could imagine how they would react. Plus, once they heard, he could kiss goodbye to keeping his findings under wrap.

Kelly picked up the phone and swore under his breath as he dialed the number Sandy had given him. He regretted promising this big-city policeman he'd meet with him and his friends. *Who the hell are they, anyway?* Kelly was a tracker and preferred to work alone, but the local sheriff had changed all of that. The phone kept ringing. Just when he was about to hang up, Sandy came on the other end.

Shit! he mouthed to the empty room.

"Hello, is there anyone there? Kelly? Is that you?"

Kelly sighed. "How'd you know it was me?"

"You're the only one I've given this number to."

At least he's careful, Kelly thought and asked, "Have you guys eaten yet?"

"We were waiting for your call."

"Okay, how about we get together at a little burger place just up the 299 from where you're staying?"

"Sure, what's it called?"

"The Early Bird. It's the home of the Bigfoot Burger." Kelly waited for a response and finally asked, "You still there?"

"The Bigfoot Burger?" Sandy chuckled. "We sure don't want to miss that."

"We can sit outside and have some privacy. How about we meet in an hour or so?"

"Copy that. See you there."

***

Sandy stared at the burger a young waitress had flopped in front of him. It smelled delicious, but he couldn't stop staring at the bun. It was shaped like a bigfoot footprint, toes and all. The young girl proudly informed him that the French buns were shaped and baked on the premises every morning.

When the girl had left, Ranger Kelly chuckled and asked, "So how do you like our local delicacy and this little hangout?"

Sandy took in the surroundings. The front of the store and restaurant were painted a bright yellow and included a cartoon-like mural of Bigfoot. He thought it an odd contrast between what he and his colleagues were investigating and this comical representation.

"People come from all over for a taste of the Bigfoot experience," Kelly said. He nodded at the mural. "Some take it more seriously than others."

"It appears so." Sandy took a large bite.

Kelly grinned and dove into his order of Bigfoot Burger and fries.

"So is this place any good?" Bobby said as he walked up to their table. "I'm starving."

They paused but continued to chew. Sandy noted the rest of the crew ambling over and returned to his meal without answering.

Kelly took in the little person. He was perfectly proportioned, just tiny, like the size of a small child. He wondered what was the proper term: midget, dwarf, or little person? He figured he'd find out soon enough.

"Well, I guess that's answer enough," Bobby said, and he led the way as Ken, Fred, and Hunt queued up behind him to place an order.

A short while later, they were all munching on their food.

"Not bad. They're not as good as Frank's, but not bad," Fred said with a smirk. "And I like the presentation. A bigfoot foot, no less."

Ken downed the last gulp from a bottle of Red Tail Ale. "And they serve a decent beer."

Bobby jumped up and headed back inside, shouting over his shoulder, "I'll get us another round. Don't decide anything until I get back."

Sandy smiled as he watched Bobby be swallowed up into a crowd of off-shift loggers. The little man ignored their amusement at his expense.

He soon returned, cradling several beers in his arms. Mark and Sandy helped him place the drinks on the table. Bobby waited until everyone had settled, then nodded to Ken.

Ken cleared his throat and smiled at Kelly. "I think it's time for us to come clean with you."

Kelly shifted in his chair. "I thought you might know more about the situation out in the forest than you've been letting on."

"We do. Or at least, we think we do."

Bobby interrupted. "Oh hell, why don't we just say it?" He waited for someone to speak but grew impatient, so continued, "The fact of the matter is we think those government types, or whatever they are, have let some big ape-like creatures loose in your backyard." Bobby nodded toward the dense forest that surrounded the little café.

"You mean like gorillas?" Kelly asked.

"Worse," Ken said.

Fred leaned toward him. "Way worse. Let's just say, for now, they're a hybrid between some really big apes, and they're very dangerous. We don't know for sure, but you finding that plane wreckage and the massacre seem more than coincidental."

Before Kelly could respond, Ken jumped in and added, "We've been chasing this mystery all over the world. Suffice it to say, we've landed here. The people associated with these hybrids are very dangerous—more dangerous than the creatures, and that's saying a lot."

Kelly couldn't contain himself any longer. "What's this have to do with Bigfoot?"

"We don't know," Ken replied. "But if Bigfoot exists, these hybrids are wandering in the same forest."

"Which could get very interesting, to say the least," Fred added.

The group talked late into the evening, unaware that the

evening crowd was thinning out and the Early Bird Café was about to close. They filled Kelly in as much as they were comfortable sharing, but they still left much out, for now.

***

"So we're in agreement, then?" Ken asked as he picked at the last crumbs of his apple pie.

"Let me get this straight," Bobby said. "We're going to traipse off into the woods with this Jimmy Two-Feathers character again while Kelly, here, takes a look around that new primate facility they're building?"

Ken nodded as he searched Kelly's face. "He's the only person here unknown to Vandusen or any of his cronies." He paused to let that sink in with everyone. To his relief, everyone nodded. "Plus, he knows the territory, and is a professional tracker. And don't forget Africa. The last time we tried to sneak into a facility, we got caught. I say we leave the checking out of that facility to a professional."

"So what do you say, Kelly?" Bobby asked.

He shrugged. "If you're right about the possibility of this facility having something to do with what happened to those poor families and that plane crash, I'll take a look around." He kept his voice down since people were passing their table, some stopping to say good night.

A young lady circulated around the tables, extinguishing candles. The full moon dropped behind the hills that ringed the town, leaving only the lengthening moon shadows.

The group sat engrossed in their own thoughts until jarred back by the loud hacking of Hunt's coughing fit. Several parties looked up from their tables as Bobby helped Hunt to the washroom.

"Is he all right?" Kelly asked as he watched Hunt stumble despite Bobby helping him across the patio.

The others watched in silence as Bobby and Hunt disappeared into the shadows around the corner.

"He's fine," Fred said. "He must've choked on something."

Ken tapped his palm on the table. "Let's get back to business."

Kelly nodded. "I'll do some poking around while you guys are out with Jimmy Two-Feathers. I should have something by the time you get back."

"Just be careful," Ken said. "You don't want to get on the wrong end of these guys."

As they made their way out of the patio, Ken caught up to Sandy and whispered, "I need you to head back to Reno and get Mary and Consuelo in the loop. Someone on the outside needs to know that we're headed out with this Jimmy Two-Feathers." Ken paused and took Sandy's arm. "I wish I knew where the hell we're headed." He frowned and started to say something, but hesitated.

Sandy looked around and watched the waitress as she busied herself stacking chairs and wiping tables. The streets were dark, absent streetlights. He leaned toward Ken. "What's wrong? What is it?"

"Don't tell the others, but I want you to contact Lester and Dusty as well. It's time to bring Oliver and Danny up here."

"And do what with them?"

"Just tell them I want them up here but under wraps. Bring one of Chris's trailers. And have them stay out of sight until I figure this out. Just say I've got a feeling they're not safe down there anymore. You can leave word with the head trainer to get Danny and Oliver ready to travel."

The two stood staring at each other. Sandy started to say something, but Bobby broke the silence. "Are you guys coming or not?"

Ken smiled, then tapped Sandy on the shoulder as they made their way down the dark street. "Just do it."

Bobby looked back and asked, "Do what?"

Ken shook his head and motioned them toward their vehicle.

Chapter Sixteen

Jimmy Two-Feathers' Ford Bronco bucked and swayed as they made their way up the dirt ranger road. He watched in the rearview mirror as Ken and the rest of the group hung onto whatever they could grab to steady themselves. No one spoke, fearing they would bite their tongues. That is, except for him. As he fought the wheel, he sang a childhood song, chanting in his own language, knowing his passengers wouldn't understand. He had trouble dodging the rocks and deep, wheel-eating furrows that scattered the road. The trees closed in around them, and the road narrowed into a two-track trail. The bouncing worsened as they climbed a steep rise. He couldn't tell if the road was as bad as it seemed or if it was just his Bronco's shot shocks and springs from years of traveling these backcountry roads.

Bobby yelled as they reach the top of the rise, "Stop, for Chrissakes!"

Jimmy slammed on the brakes, filling the Bronco with a cloud of dust through the open windows.

Between coughing spasms, Hunt yelled, "Open the goddamn door!" He pushed Fred out and stood, stomping his feet and dusting himself off before he leaned forward, holding his knees, and vomited. They watched as Hunt weakly straightened and wiped his face with a handkerchief.

"Are you okay, Hunt?" Fred asked.

"What do you think?"

Bobby looked from Fred to the others and whispered to Fred, "Do you think Hunt can make it? The others don't know how sick he is."

Fred squinted and whispered, "It's up to Hunt to tell the others, not us."

Bobby nodded and brought Hunt a towel.

Jimmy propped the hood up to let the engine cool while these palefaces rested. He was used to tourists and their idiosyncrasies, but this group was different. He found a rock to rest his butt on and waited, wondering what Bobby and Fred were being so secretive about.

Ken walked over to Jimmy and asked, "How much further is it to this cave of yours?"

"A ways. We can camp here tonight."

Ken looked at Hunt and said loud enough for everyone to hear, "We're setting up camp here for the night."

No one said anything as they began unpacking the Bronco.

***

Darkness filled the forest, and a chill settled in the air. They hoped they'd gathered enough firewood to last the evening. Jimmy had made it clear they shouldn't wander too far from camp. He'd whispered when he'd warned, "This is Ohmah country. Stay in sight of one another."

They learned that he was a member of the Hupa tribe, and his people believed that Ohmah, or Bigfoot, still walked this forest, especially along where the Trinity and Klamath Rivers met. They'd asked Jimmy to guide them to Bluff Creek—the place Patterson and Gimli had filmed a female bigfoot.

"Our grandparents warned us, when we were children, not to wander too far from the village when the sun set, as Ohmah might kidnap us," Jimmy said. "We didn't believe them at first—until it happened." He threw another log on the campfire, raising sparks. "Once, when I was very young, I was fishing with my brother when the darkness caught us. The fishing had been good, and we wanted to surprise our parents with our bounty." The group waited, saying nothing, as Jimmy softly chanted while looking up at the sky.

"So what happened?" Bobby asked, not sure if the chill he felt came from the growing darkness or the tale Jimmy was telling them.

Jimmy frowned. "As we gathered the last of our nets at the water's edge, a large boulder landed near our canoe. It just missed us. The boulder was as big as half the canoe. And then we heard cries . . . Cries like we'd never heard before." He paused. "We were sure something had thrown it at us, and the cries were unworldly, like spirits." He began quietly chanting again.

The campfire threw shadows that danced off the group's faces. They looked around, trying to pierce the darkness, and jumped when a screech owl disturbed the quiet of the night.

"It could've been a rockslide or something," Bobby said.

"It was more like something." Jimmy stretched out his legs and leaned back in his canvas chair. "The boulders were huge, bigger than three men could lift, and they landed all around us, like someone was aiming them at us. One hit our canoe and folded it in half."

The group sat in silence, sometimes looking up at the stars.

Eventually, Jimmy spoke again. "We are intruders here. This is Ohmah's land."

Bobby stood abruptly, startling them. "Thanks for the

bedtime story, Jimmy." He stretched for a long while before saying, "Well, I'm going to try to catch some Zs, if that's possible."

He laid out his sleeping bag near the fire and rolled over, his back to the rest of them. Each followed suit, finding a place to unroll their bags and mats and bed down. The babbling of the river and the crackling of the fire lulled them to sleep, leaving them to their thoughts and then dreams. They couldn't help but think of Africa and how many times they'd slept together around a fire, hoping to see the morning.

***

"Did you hear that?" Bobby yelled, sitting up still wrapped in his mummy bag.

The rest stirred around the dying embers of what was left of their campfire. Ken rubbed the sleep out of his eyes. "Where's our guide?"

They looked at Jimmy's empty sleeping bag. Bobby shone his flashlight to make sure the Bronco was still there. The full moon sat low on the horizon, illuminating the distant peaks. All was still.

"Quit pointing that damn thing at me," Hunt said, shading his eyes.

"Where did that damn Indian go?" Bobby asked.

Hunt picked up a hatchet. "I wish Sandy was with us. At least he'd have a gun."

"It'll be dawn soon," Fred said, looking at the illuminated dials of his watch.

Ken threw the remaining logs and kindling on the fire while Bobby stoked it. The rest pulled their chairs in closer but turned them outward to face the darkness. Just as the first light of dawn swallowed the darkness, a loud whistle broke the silence of the woods. They looked at each other before saying anything. Several cries, as though answering it, echoed off the distant hills.

"What the hell is that?" Hunt asked, gripping the hatchet tighter.

"Shh!" Ken put his finger to his lips.

The forest was silent for several heartbeats before a chorus of cries and whistles brought in the first light of dawn.

They'd just decided to head to the Bronco when the cries ceased and left them with only the morning breeze to disturb their thoughts.

Bobby looked out from the open door and asked, "Does anyone know how to hot-wire this piece of crap?"

"No need for that." Jimmy stepped into the clearing, holding the keys above his head.

"Where the hell have you been?" Ken asked.

"I left an offering for Ohmah."

"You what?" Fred asked.

"I left a jar of peanut butter and some oranges for them," Jimmy replied.

They stood staring at each other. Jimmy rolled up his sleeping bag, and the rest followed without a word.

***

Ken and crew were relieved when Jimmy pulled back onto the trail and drove the Bronco deeper into the forest. He'd promised to show them some Hupa rock art that depicted Bigfoot—or so he said. They couldn't have the AC on, for fear of overheating, so the dust settled in clouds that covered everything and everyone inside. They drove for hours, until all but Jimmy had lost their bearings. Only the sun gave them any hint of the direction in which they were headed. Just when they thought they couldn't take another bump or turn, Jimmy stopped the Bronco. They tumbled out, grateful for the reprieve. Ken stretched and tried to walk off his fatigue. The rest followed his lead.

Without saying anything, Jimmy motioned them to follow. They scrambled up a steep hillside littered with loose rocks. The slope steepened so much that they had to crawl the last stage to reach the jagged outcrop Jimmy indicated. The sun beat down, roasting everything in the open, and there was an absence of birds or other wildlife. It was a relief to reach the shade of the rocks, where water wept from the cracks, hinting at a spring. The aroma of sage filled the air.

Fred was the first to see Jimmy bowing, his lips whispering as he kneeled before a giant petroglyph of a stick man. When his eyes adjusted to the shade, he noticed that etchings covered the whole face of the boulder. Some were small, humanlike figures standing next to figures twice as tall. Others showed the smaller figures holding spears next to deer and other animals. It was obvious they were standing next to a very old and sacred place.

Fred touched Jimmy on the shoulder and asked, "What is this place?"

Jimmy stirred as though out of a trance. "This is the story of Ohmah."

Bobby reached to trace his finger on one of the drawings, but Jimmy pulled him back. "The spirits are alive here. Don't touch anything. We're guests."

Bobby open his mouth to say something but thought better of it and stepped away from the rocks.

"What does all this mean, Jimmy?" Ken asked.

"Ohmah has lived in this forest since before my people came to this land," he replied.

"Who made these drawings?"

"The ancestors of my people. But come over here."

They followed Jimmy to a cave opening hidden by the outcrop but hesitated before entering into the darkness. Jimmy pulled a flashlight out of a rawhide pouch slung over his shoulder, and they followed him inside and looked around.

Above their heads several life-size figures of humanlike creatures adorned the rock. And below them was a smaller cluster of two figures over six.

Bobby squinted at the drawings. "We've seen this arrangement before."

Hunt nodded. "Dr. Raven's ranch, the piece of bark on the beach in Africa, on the cage wall at that dark little carnival in the Black Forest. What was it called?" He paused for a moment, thinking. "Ah yes, Steinwasen. And now here."

"There's more." Jimmy pointed at a drawing on the other wall of the cave. "This is new."

They gathered around what seemed to be a newly carved drawing. The lines were fresh, and a pointed rock lay on the ground near it.

"Two lines over six," Ken said.

Jimmy frowned. "These drawings weren't made by my people."

Chapter Seventeen

Lester stood at the front door of his trailer and took a final look around. Girlie ambled down the hallway and did a somersault onto the worn couch. She looked quizzical and signed, "Go now?"

The old man wondered how many times he and his chimp Girlie had stood on the threshold or stoop somewhere, ready for the next show or adventure. It changed after his wife, Karen, had passed, but just the same, they were heading out and that suited him just fine. He'd lost touch with his friends after their return to the States around six months ago. He'd thought, at the time, that Africa and their adventure might kill him and Girlie, but it'd done just the opposite. New life had coursed through his veins and Girlie had pranced like an adolescent chimp again.

How old were they? he wondered. He counted the circuses and shows in which they'd performed, quietly moving his lips, and decided he must be in his seventies and Girlie close to sixty. He'd fallen back into that life-sucking routine of staying in his trailer with his old chimp, Girlie, the last of his act, surrounded by haunting memories. He missed being on the road, going from one jump to another. He missed not knowing what each day would bring, but he missed Karen the most. They'd been center-ring royalty once, but now he was just an old man nobody remembered except at the Circus Luncheon Club.

Lester smiled while petting Girlie. "Yes, we're going now. Hurry!" He lifted his luggage with a moan and motioned Girlie to follow. Someone was honking a horn. He sighed and yelled, "All right, all right, already. We're coming."

Hooting, Girlie raced past him toward Dusty, who stood next to the open door of a rusty Willys Jeep Station Wagon. He smiled and said, "Hello, old friend."

"Hello, yourself," Lester said as he struggled to drag two suitcases down the steps.

"I didn't mean you, you old son of a bitch," Dusty replied with a smirk.

"Who you calling old?" Lester asked, furrowing his brow.

"Well, I sure don't mean Girlie, here." Dusty laughed as he untangled himself from her embrace.

Lester couldn't help but notice how stout and stocky Dusty was, a typical elephant trainer. His thick frame moved with slow but deliberate steps. Lester couldn't count how many shows they'd worked on together. For all their differences, especially over Oliver, he was a man you could count on in a pinch.

"Girlie, give us a hand!" Lester yelled, pausing at the bottom step.

***

Dusty followed Girlie as she raced to pull one of the suitcases from Lester's grip. Dusty picked up the other without another word. He noticed Girlie seemed bonier than the last time he'd seen her, and Lester definitely moved slower. He hoped they were up for this trip, especially after all he'd learned from Fred. Everything had gone back to normal since they worked themselves free of Vandusen and his gang. They'd not heard or seen them in close to six months. But now, all of a sudden, Ken and his crowd were worried and going to stir the pot again. And all because of those damn freaks of nature. He opened his mouth to comment, but shut it and busied himself rearranging stacks in the back of the Willys.

It took several stuttering turns before the old Willys Jeep spat into life, coughing and spewing black smoke. Dust and rust rained down on their heads as they jerked into motion.

Lester brushed a hand through his hair and glared at Dusty. "Do you think this old wreck will make it to Reno?"

Ignoring him, Dusty floored it, jerking their heads back and forth as he finally found third gear with a grind. Girlie hooted and bounced in the back seat, trying to find a pitch higher than the whining engine.

Lester knew it was better not to say any more but couldn't help himself. "What the hell?" he yelled.

Dusty looked over at him, smiling, and gave the gas pedal another boost.

"So what couldn't you share on the phone?" Lester asked. "All I know is that Ken asked us to head up to Reno to help with 'the big chimps.' By which, I figure, he means Oliver and Danny."

"Yeah. He wants us to get them ready to move," Dusty said. "He doesn't think it'll be safe for them in Reno for much longer. He thinks they're being watched, again."

"Where to?"

"That's the big question," Dusty replied. "I guess he'll let us know when he's figured it out."

***

Lester couldn't believe they'd stopped again as he stepped out of Dusty's relic of a vehicle and tried to stretch the stiffness out of his joints. He noticed the hood up and walked around to find Dusty pouring in a can of Castro. Lester leaned over to get a better look. "Damn, this piece of shit is sure thirsty."

Dusty ignored him as he threw the empty oilcan in the bushes and shoved the rusty oil spout into another can.

A whole case of cans lay at his feet, so Lester thought it might be a good time to take Girlie for a walk, but he thought better of it when he noticed her still sleeping in the back. He hoped she'd be up for this trip. He wasn't too sure how long they'd be away.

An idea kept turning in his head, one he knew was crazy, but what the hell. He'd wait for the right time to pitch it, which, knowing Dusty, would probably need to be over dinner.

The 101 was cold and damp, and he figured they must be getting close to the Pacific coast by now. He wasn't sure how long he'd slept before this stop, but from looking around at the rolling hills of oaks and the dusty ranches on the hillsides, he figured they must be somewhere near Atascadero or Paso Robles. They still had a long way to go, and even longer if Dusty went for his idea.

Lester looked around again as Dusty screwed the oil-filler cap back on the head and wiped his hands on his overalls. His beefy hands covered most of the can's label. The sun was at that time of day which they called, in the movies, the magic hour. His wife, Karen, had always loved this time. The hills blazed golden, and the eastern sky grew azure as the sun disappeared behind the coastal hills. It was times like these that he missed Karen the most. *How long has it been?*

Dusty slammed the hood, and Girlie stirred from under her blanket and signed, "Out."

Lester took her hand and scrambled down below the highway to a small creek that fed a trickle to a sparse grove of willows and sycamores. He could just hear Dusty holler, "Be careful of stinging nettles!"

Lester was tempted to yell what he thought of Dusty's warning but decided to ignore his remark. He followed the creek until he found a clearing where Girlie could safely exercise out of sight of any pain-in-the-ass looky-loos. He watched her chase some blackbirds as though she hadn't a care in the world, and he realized that at this moment, she didn't. From all the years he'd been in the company of chimps, it never ceased to amaze him that they were much better at remaining in the present moment than humans. He envied her lack of anxiety. How wonderful it must be not to worry about the consequences of your decisions.

He thought again of what he wanted to suggest to Dusty. A plan that didn't stop at Reno. He wasn't sure why he even wanted to go there now, after refusing when Ken had invited him right after they returned from their adventures. But now he felt an urgency to check on Oliver and Danny. In fact, some of the old anxiety of their travels was returning. Several times, he'd noticed a vehicle parked down the street from his house, and the last time he'd gone to the Luncheon Club, he thought he'd seen that sedan again—or was he just being paranoid?

Girlie was the first to notice the sound of a vehicle pulling into the wide spot in the road where they'd stopped. She stared up the hillside toward the jeep, then when they heard two doors slam and the gravel crunching under footsteps, she jumped and grimaced, showing all her teeth. Before Lester could reach her, she raced up the hill.

He tried to catch up with Girlie, but it was useless. He could hear her grunts as she bounded to the crest of the road cut, leaped over the guardrail and disappeared from sight. Shouting and screaming rose up, echoing off the hillsides, and then silence. Lester was breathless when he reached the top of the hill and climbed over the wooden railing. Below him, two men lay motionless beside the Willys with Dusty and Girlie riffling through their clothing.

Dusty looked up from his work and said, "Nice of you to make it."

"What the hell happened?" Lester asked as he leaned over, arms on his thighs, trying to catch his breath.

"What's it look like?" Dusty held out two pistols. "Girlie got here just in time."

Girlie grabbed the pistols, raced over to Lester, and dropped them at his feet.

"Good girl," Lester said as he picked them up by the butts. He held them between his thumb and forefinger and took a closer look.

"Quick!" Dusty said as he rummaged through the back of the Willys. "Let's tie them up before we have to put them down again. We're lucky no one has come by yet. We can call the police when we get a long way from here."

Girlie watched without expression, then raced over to the back seat and pulled a roll of duct tape out of a toolbox.

"Where in the hell did she learn that, d'you suppose?" Dusty asked, wrinkling his forehead.

"Where do you think? Africa," Lester said in a low voice. "Make sure you leave space for them to breathe," he added in a whisper.

Dusty looked up from his work. "Why?"

Lester just shook his head.

With the help of Girlie, they bound and gagged the men, and dragged the two limp bodies back to the men's black sedan.

As they closed the car doors, Lester said, "Now tell me.

What the hell happened here?"

"Well, it all happened pretty fast," Dusty replied. "These guys showed up and were reaching for guns when Girlie took them both down to the ground in a fuckin' blur. I hit one of them with this oilcan and Girlie took care of the other." He picked up a bent and leaking Castro can. "If she hadn't shown up and acted so quickly, I don't know what would've happened. Christ! This is way too weird."

"Well, let's not wait for them to wake up. This looks like the same car that parked down from my place several times last week. I say we haul ass and disappear before someone shows up." Lester took Girlie's hand and headed back to the Willys.

Dusty nodded. "Right, we've been lucky so far. We can make a call at the first greaser we find."

Lester smiled at the word *greaser*. It was a term circus people used for a place to eat. *Besides making that call, we can talk about my idea.*

Chapter Eighteen

The Congo, present day

François waited outside the infirmary for the medic to finish his rounds. He couldn't bring himself to go inside anymore. Most of the native women they'd rescued, if *rescued* was the proper word, had been lost. They were dead. In the months after their attack on the caves, they'd watched in horror as each woman died in labor. The soldiers who'd been part of the raid rarely talked about what they'd found. But that didn't change what they'd seen and were seeing with each attempted birth. Fortunately, the abominations that had grown in their wombs died as well.

The Belgians had been busy since Lester had left, and François missed him. They'd become close during the months they'd fought side by side to keep the creatures safe from Vandusen and his renegades. François didn't regret staying in Africa. Any doubts he'd had about his decision to stay were forgotten after what they'd discovered at the caves.

François had had little time to think of anything but the building of a new compound. He and his men had made a Herculean effort to salvage equipment and materials from the ruins of their old compound and move it deeper into the jungle to a location far up the Congo River, a more secluded area. They'd had to move under the cover of darkness to avoid being detected by prying eyes. On top of that, during the occupation of their old compound, Vandusen had forced them into the jungle during the day, which had put them at the mercy of the relentless tsetse fly. Many of his men were now suffering from sleeping sickness as a result. He was slightly comforted when he found several of Vandusen's men suffering from the dreaded disease. Sleeping sickness and snail fever were the scourge of Africa.

François stirred from his thoughts at the sound of the medic's footsteps on the wooden deck. Looking up, he asked, "So what's the verdict, Doc?"

Doc furrowed his brow and looked over his shoulder back toward the screen door. "We lost another one. I don't think any of them will come to term."

"I'm not sure that's a bad thing, Doc."

Doc exhaled loudly and leaned against the railing where François propped his boots before saying, "I'm a combat medic, sir. I can patch gunshot wounds and take care of the illnesses that the jungle brings, but I've no training or experience with this sort of thing."

François could see that Doc was beaten. He'd watched his medic try to save the women, but most had died. Only ten had survived the long trek from the caves to their new compound, but now they were down to three. The poor women lay sweating from fever and writhing in pain from the growing seeds in their wombs. They'd been through unspeakable things.

Doc had aged before his time. The Congo had a way of doing that to outsiders, especially Europeans. The poor man was fading. His blond hair was thinning, and his khakis hung loosely on the rack of his frame. His eyes sank deep into the hollows above his cheeks, and his voice had grown old. But he was their only hope, since their real doctor had left months before under the cover of Chris and the film crew. François wondered if they'd ever get another MD back again, especially after all that had happened. Their communication back to the real world was broken, and he wasn't sure if they would ever get it reestablished.

He looked up, realizing Doc still stood there as though waiting for an answer. But François had no answers. "What is it, Doc?" he asked.

"I don't think any of these women can deliver on their own."

François sensed that the medic wanted to say more.

Doc shifted his weight between his feet, causing him to sway, but he said nothing more.

Finally, François broke the silence. "So what do we do?"

"Without a physician, I'm not sure."

"We've always counted on you in the field, Doc."

"Well, this is way beyond what I know. If these women can't deliver naturally, they're gonna die. It's as simple as that."

"So we'll have to operate?" François asked.

"*We* don't have the training, sir."

François paced the patio while Doc watched. Finally, François turned and said, "I'm sorry, but you're going to have to operate. You're going to have to do— what do they call it?—a cesarean."

Doc nodded and left for the library without a word.

***

The medic walked across the compound, dodging puddles of water. He pulled his hood over to keep the drizzle out of his eyes. Work had slowed for the rainy season, but the library was

122

nearing completion. He smiled to himself as he entered the Quonset hut. This medical library was a far cry from Oxford, but it was probably the best for a thousand miles around. Volumes had been collected over the years, and they'd survived Vandusen's attack.

An orderly looked up, pausing from opening large crates of books that were lined up in front of tall shelves. Each crate was stenciled with the names of its contents: *Tropical Medicine, Neurology, Anesthesiology*, and most importantly, *Obstetrics and Gynecology*.

Doc kneeled and began stacking books and journals into groups. An orderly lit a kerosene lamp and set it next to him. Doc nodded after picking up a volume. He looked up at the orderly and read the title. "*Taber's Cyclopedic Medical Dictionary*." He set the lantern close beside him, picked up a magnifying glass, and carefully leafed through the thin, delicate pages. "Here we are, the cesarean section." He leaned closer to the lantern, magnifying glass in hand. The orderly stepped aside as to not cast a shadow. Doc read for several minutes, pausing to write notes. The orderly soon lost interest and returned to cataloging.

Doc's reading brought back memories of lectures long ago, in another part of the world, on childbirth and the complications that could occur. As he read about the cesarean section, he realized his first choice was between a conservative or a radical approach, one in which the uterus would or would not be removed. He stood up and walked to the window and watched some workmen building boardwalks between the newly constructed buildings. His main goal was to save those poor women. Only three remained. He read on, not noticing François slipping in to check on him. His next choice was between "absolute" or "relative." He exhaled loud enough for the orderly to look up from his work. He read some more.

"Finally!" he yelled to no one in particular. He motioned the orderly over and began to read. "Here we are. 'C. S., relative. Where the child could be delivered through the natural passages, but where such a delivery might jeopardize the life of the mother or the child.' That's our problem. And listen to this—there are at least two reasons to perform a relative cesarean: 'A large baby with a moderate degree of disproportion,' and 'Preeclamptic toxemia in patients where a difficult labor is anticipated.'" He nodded at the orderly. "We're going to take a radical approach. It's our only hope."

Doc noticed François and said, "I'll make a list. We're going to need some special forceps and lots of suturing supplies. The little bit of catgut I have on hand isn't going to fly."

François nodded and reached for the door, but Doc called after him, "Wait! We don't have enough ether." Doc paused and picked up another volume. "I'll make an incision down the abdomen, move the bladder out of the way and then open the uterus. That's going to take a lot of ether and sutures."

François frowned. "I'll get on the radio."

"See if you can get a real doctor, while you're at it!" Doc yelled.

François left the library without a word.

Chapter Nineteen

Tamara thought about calling Fred, but she'd heard from some of his students that he'd already left town. So that left Mary, but she wasn't sure what to tell her. Everyone she trusted had apparently left with Dr. Turner for the little town of Willow Creek up in Northern California. She was sure it had to do with what he'd asked her to investigate a few weeks before. She thought about his recent visit and how interested he'd been in Bigfoot. While she'd shared that there'd been sightings of these creatures all over the world, he seemed most interested in those near where the campers had been massacred and the girls abducted. The description in the newspaper unnerved her. The images were horrific, reminding her of what she'd read about the Charles Manson murders.

After putting the pieces together, she now suspected that the reason Fred had asked her to keep Dr. Ken Turner's interest in Bigfoot a secret wasn't that he didn't want to be scorned by the scientific community but that he thought there might be some connection between Bigfoot and those hideous creatures in the photos from Africa.

Dr. Turner had been most interested in the Patterson-Gimli film she'd shown him. He'd replayed the frames of the creature looking back over its shoulder several times. Before leaving, he'd asked her to investigate all the sightings of Bigfoot in the Willow Creek/Trinity Wilderness area and map them out. Her findings disturbed her.

She leaned back in her chair and looked up at the map of California she had pinned on the wall above her desk. Red pins marked every sighting of Bigfoot in the last ninety years. She'd numbered each pin marker to correspond to a description of the sightings. The densest cluster of pins was around the Willow Creek area. Now that she knew Dr. Turner and his team were up in that very area, she needed to get the notes of these sightings to him as soon as possible.

Something wasn't right. In all the descriptions of encounters with Bigfoot, and there were hundreds around the Willow Creek area, it was rare that these creatures had been violent. While there'd been disappearances, nothing had been like what had happened to those poor campers. Several sightings coincided with the arrival home of Dr. Turner and his colleagues from Africa. But the details of those sightings were different. Instead of retreating into the woods, these creatures had attacked. They'd been aggressive rather than reclusive, and there'd been at least a dozen incidents building up to the massacre.

She leafed through her notes again and thought back to her first visit to Dr. Turner's facility, when Mary had called her in to look at the photographs of Africa. How long ago had that been? She flipped through a calendar on her desk. Over six months had passed, but it seemed longer. It suddenly dawned on her that maybe Africa had come to visit Willow Creek! Dr. Turner had been looking for the creatures she'd seen in those old photographs. He must have found them and brought them back from Africa, but somehow they'd gotten loose in the wilds surrounding Willow Creek. *But how?*

Tamara pushed her chair back from her desk and spun around on its wheels—a habit of hers when thinking. She looked back up at the map and noticed a blue pin in the cluster of red. She stood to get a closer look at the number flagged on it and thumbed through her notebook. The Department of Defense was setting up a research center a few miles outside of Willow Creek, in an old logging camp. But why there? It had to have something to do with those recent incidents, or worse, the massacre. Agents of the government had been pursuing Turner and his crew in Africa. Did they have something to do with these mysterious events up north?

She banged on the bent file drawer several times to get it to open and pulled out the file corresponding to the number flagged on the pin. It was coming back to her now. She hadn't thought much about a facility being opened by the government up there until now. She gathered her notes and, with her Polaroid, took a picture of the maps she'd created. It was time to head up to Willow Creek. Hopefully her VW Bug would make the drive.

But she'd call Mary first.

Tamara hesitated before picking up the phone, but she felt committed now. She looked again at Mary's phone number, which Dr. Turner had scribbled on his business card, and paused with her finger on the dial. If she spun the last number, there'd be no turning back. She took a deep breath and let it spin. It only rang twice before she heard Mary's clear voice on the other end.

"Hello?"

"Is this Mary?" Tamara asked.

"Who is this?"

Tamara paused as she tried to pick her words. She cursed to herself for not planning what she was going to say. She wiped her forehead with the back of her hand. It felt sticky. Her heart raced. She had to say something and break the silence. She could hear the faint background noise of someone fumbling with something on the other end. Finally, she took a deep breath and said, "Ah, this is Tamara, Mark's friend. Remember me? I helped you a little while ago with those photos from the Congo that Dr. Turner was researching." There was a long pause. Tamara was losing her nerve and was about to hang up when Mary finally answered.

"Yes, this is Mary. I remember you. What can I do for you?"

Tamara wasn't sure she should've called. Mary's voice sounded flat, as though she was trying to suppress her emotions. Maybe even suspicious.

What have I got myself into? Tamara wondered.

"Are you there?"

Tamara looked up at the map, took a breath and said, "I've been doing some more research for your husband and Fred, or I should say Dr. Savage, and think I have information that could help them. I've been plotting the locations of all the sightings—"

"Not on the phone, dear. Let's meet . . ."

Tamara waited silently during the long pause before Mary continued.

"Let's meet where we first met—don't answer. Just think where we met—say, at one this afternoon? You know, not at the library, but when we were looking at that package we shared with you."

"Got it, Mary."

"Good, and be sure to come alone. Make sure you're not being followed. It's been crazy ever since the hearing, you know."

Tamara realized that Mary's concern had nothing to do with the hearing. She felt herself being pulled into something far more sinister than press photographers or some university administrators. She picked her words carefully, realizing that

Mary didn't want to say too much over the phone. "I'll be there, like last time."

"See you this afternoon, then."

Tamara held the receiver, listening to the dial tone and wondering what all this secrecy meant. Just as she was about to hang up, she thought she heard a faint click.

"Hello? . . . Hello?" Her only answer was the usual static of an open line.

She hung up the phone and stared into space for several heartbeats. The basement boiler startled her when it kicked in, rattling the duct work above her. Her office walls seemed to close in around her. She rotated her head, trying to relax the muscles in her neck, her long blond hair falling across her face. Even reaching back with her hands and massaging her shoulders with her fingers didn't work. Nothing did.

The entry door buzzer echoed through the stacks, making her jump, but she stopped just before pressing the button on the intercom. *Who would be calling at this hour?* Her heart began to race. She looked around, taking an inventory of what she needed to take with her. She grabbed her keys, but just as she was about to shut the door, she turned back and tore the map she'd so carefully prepared off the wall. The pins scattered across her desk. She locked her office door and raced toward the fire exit, smiling at the prospect of setting off the alarm.

Chapter Twenty

Kelly stretched his arms up well above his head. He ached from hours of standing in the cold, watching the facility below. He remembered when it had been a bustling logging camp employing half the town of Willow Creek. *How long has it been?* he wondered. His father had worked there, trucking logs every day to Eureka. The place had changed since then. Now it was a ghost town of rusting equipment and piles of rotting logs. He still didn't understand why the government would pick this remote location for an animal research facility. The fog thickened as evening settled on the forest. The first work lights startled him, casting a hazy glow that cloaked everything from view. *What are they doing down there, especially on a cold, foggy night like this?*

He'd positioned himself to have a clear view of the only road going in and out. Trucks and vans hauling building supplies and workers had been coming and going all day. He could hear more down there than he could see. That was the funny thing about fog. It seemed to amplify sounds. A closing door miles away could be heard as though it was right next to you. As the fog thickened, he heard muffled voices, coughs, and laughs. He gathered there were a lot of people down there. He picked up his pack and struggled through the manzanita and blackberry thickets that had replaced the old growth. The area surrounding the camp below had been clear-cut, making it almost impossible to negotiate. The hoots of a great horned owl seemed to mark his steps.

A tall wire fence topped with ribbon wire traced the perimeter. A clearing the width of a football field aproned it. He stopped at a shorter fence at its edge. The whole place looked more like a military installation than a research facility. *If this was Nam, I'd say that's a minefield.* He froze as he spied a soldier walking along the inside fence. He waited for his eyes to adjust to the bright lights streaming from the interior of the compound. This dense fog and the glow of those lights was a bad mix. *What does a research facility need with the military?*

He was on edge more than usual. The whole business of the massacre and meeting that out-of-town detective—what was his name?—Sandy had got him thinking. And then there was that whole episode during his tracking. *What was that all about, that footprint and the cries and the rock throwing and the markings?* Something was afoot he didn't like. He checked himself. His mind was wandering and not attending to the business at hand. In his past life in Vietnam, that could get you killed. He needed to get closer. So far he could only see dark silhouettes moving through the thick fog.

A chorus of sharp, inhuman, primal cries disrupted the night. He threw himself flat. These cries were different from the ones he'd heard before. More savage. A chill passed over his already chilled body. The pitch was so high it set the bats and night birds answering. It sounded like pain competing with rage. He didn't want to meet whatever or whoever was making such a sound. The sharp report of a slamming door swallowed them whole, and a few heartbeats later, all was silent but the hum of what sounded like a generator.

His instincts made him want to clear out, but it had taken him all day to get this close. He needed to take advantage of this fog and settle down. It was time to earn his pay. If he could find out what happened to those campers by investigating what was below, he would, no matter the cost. He steeled his nerves and started to low-crawl his way toward the perimeter. There had to be an opening that could give him ingress. Hell, every setup had a weak spot in its security. After all, he'd been best in his company at infiltrating back in the day, when he had been "in country."

It unnerved him that this fog seemed to telegraph every sound he made as he crawled along the edge of the fence. He hoped they didn't have dogs. Christ, he hated dogs. The Viet Cong had used them to great effect. Dogs could hear way better than the best scout. So far, so good. All he could see were guards walking the fence line, nothing more. No electronics, but best, no goddamn dogs.

Shit! The wind was coming up, and it was beginning to rain; the fog was going to clear. He'd have to pull back as soon as possible. That's when he saw it: a creek trickled out of the tree line, filling a marsh along the fence. A pile of lumber lay on the other side. He might be able to work his way along the bank and get under the two fences and hide there. There was just one problem. The clearing looked like a perfect place for landmines. He checked himself. *Am I crazy? This is fuckin' America. Nobody mines anything.* The mist was turning to rain, and the thickness of the fog tore away in patches. The weather was clearing, leaving him exposed. He had to either retreat to the cover of the forest or try to cross the clearing and take cover behind a pile of lumber.

He decided that this was his best chance to get a closer look at this place. He'd been stonewalled when he tried to get an appointment to visit, but Detective Sandy had shared what he thought was happening in those buildings behind this security fencing. Kelly pulled his Buck knife out and dug his way under the first fence. The soggy mud of the marsh made it easier than he thought. He pulled thick carpets of moss loose from under the wire, and when he could finally wiggle under it, he was careful not to make too much noise. Slowly, he picked his way across the clearing and froze when two guards stopped at the second fence and shone flashlights in his direction. He lay still, but fortunately they aimed their lights into the trees.

"I swear I heard something," a voiced whispered. "I tell you, there's something out there."

"Do you want to wait out here until the bosses come for a look?"a second voice asked. "Our shift is almost over."

Kelly waited for several minutes after the lights extinguished to be sure the guards were gone. The second fence was harder to dig under, but he was lucky. Though the fence poles had insulators, no electrical wire had been stretched yet. He took the time to fill the hole behind him and cover everything with the soggy marsh grass. When he finally reached the cover of the wood pile, he sighed. He'd once remained in a POW compound for several days and had only been able to rescue several POWs when a chance airstrike had diverted the enemy's attention long enough to crawl out. Fortunately, this facility wasn't as well guarded, but he'd need to take some time to look around. There would be no air support on this mission. For now, he needed to catch his breath.

***

Kelly lay as still as possible, watching. Workmen scurried everywhere. Some busied themselves tossing debris into piles while others repaired or constructed buildings. Hammering and sawing echoed so loud that he could only hear snippets of conversation. He'd have to get closer to the action if he wanted to eavesdrop.

Suddenly, out of the darkness, a voice asked, "Where're you supposed to be? Damnit, you're not being paid to nap!"

Kelly jumped, bolted up, and faced a man holding a rifle. He said the only thing he could think of. "Sorry, sir. I was just taking a break."

"That's not what I asked you."

Kelly pointed at a group of workers throwing anything flammable into a pile to make what looked like a bonfire. "I'm with that crew."

The man motioned him to join the group.

Kelly walked toward the group, his heart pounding so hard he thought he was having a heart attack. He made furtive glances from side to side, hoping to find a way to escape. But before he spun into action, the man said, "You boys keep an eye on this guy. He likes to take naps."

A few laughs rose up, but no one looked away from their work. Kelly thought his legs would give out. *That was way too close.*

It didn't take long before he learned that his coworkers had been hired as temporary laborers from an employment agency in Eureka out on the coast. They'd been contracted for a few weeks to help with the cleanup. Luck had treated him well, as these were the only outside people in the whole place, but their movement was restricted. A guard moved with them everywhere they went. He'd been lucky that the guard who'd caught him had been talking to one of the bosses and thought he'd just slipped off to avoid work. The only light in the area came from the fence line and cloaked them in shadows, so it'd been hard to see anything.

As Kelly helped make ready the coming bonfire, he worried that it would illuminate the area enough for the guard to recognize that the count was wrong. He had to do something soon, but he wasn't sure what.

A voice out of the shadows jarred him from his thoughts. "I need two men to help unload a couple of trucks."

The man who'd discovered Kelly pointed at him and said, "Here, be sure you take that guy who likes naps."

A guard led Kelly and another worker to a large corrugated Quonset hut where several trucks were idling. He tried to walk while holding a flashlight to a clipboard and so paid little attention to them. "Christ! This is going to take all fucking night."

They stopped under a floodlight at the double doors of the Quonset and could barely hear each other over the roar of a generator. The man shouted, "Just unload all the shit in these trucks and stack it in here." He pointed inside. "The quartermaster in there will tell you how to organize it, but be careful and don't drop any of it. This stuff's crazy expensive medical equipment." He paused, looking at Kelly, and said, "If you do a good job here, we might keep both of you on for a little while."

Kelly, following his fellow laborer, gave a broad smile.

The man nodded and said, "You can't beat this work, and it's all cash."

Someone must really like me up there, he thought. It seemed to Kelly that he'd dodged a bullet again, literally.

***

Kelly took a deep breath as he watched an orange glow tint the clouds in the eastern sky. He usually loved dawn in the forest, but he wasn't sure what this one would bring. He returned to unloading the semi, since that was his only option just now. He'd started a game he was going to have to play out. He focused on the work at hand, but the growing light gave him a chance to get a better look around. He was amazed at the transformation that had occurred in this old, run-down logging camp. The ruins had been transformed. There was new construction in every direction, but it was the fencing and towers that caught his eye the most. These people, whoever they were, were going to great lengths to make the area inside impenetrable. In a few more months, they'd succeed.

Several areas caught his eye as he surveyed his surroundings. Without being too obvious, he tried to make a mental note of the layout. It helped that he'd been inside before when visiting his father. It was very different now, but he could still get his bearings.

On the hill above sat the house where the foreman had lived in the old days, now freshly painted with an apron of lawns. Secondary fencing surrounded it and the entry gate appeared locked. He couldn't tell who lived there yet as it was early, but time would tell. At the opposite end from where he stood was a complex of buildings protected by yet another fence, this one electrified and topped with concertina wire. He soon figured out that the cries that had so unnerved him the evening before came from buildings behind the fence. A complex of old wooden barracks stood near the front entrance. These seemed to house the soldiers, who were segregated from the rest of the workers. Some, walking with purpose in every direction, looked to be scientists or doctors. Interesting. Though early, it was already a bustling place.

He leaned down to pick up another box and heard footsteps crunching the gravel behind him. He turned, struggling from the weight, and a short, pear-shaped man in a lab coat grabbed the other side. Kelly realized he was a scientist from his name tag: Dr. Melon, Senior Research Scientist. *Why does that name ring a bell?* Then it struck him—the missing person Lt. Sandy was looking for.

The man smiled and said, "I'll shake your hand when we get inside. I'm Dr. Melon."

Kelly smiled back but without thinking gave his real name.

"Good to meet you, Kelly. I wonder if you could give me a hand after we get this load inside."

Kelly nodded, knowing he'd crossed the point of no return but would just have to play the hand he had dealt himself.

***

Kelly waited as Melon filled two Styrofoam cups from a large coffee urn, then he followed Melon over to a table of donuts and pastries.

Melon pointed at the spread on the table and said, "Please help yourself."

Kelly had to control his urge to wolf down everything in sight. He couldn't remember the last time he'd had anything to eat. He'd left his backpack behind and hadn't had the opportunity to get back to it. He glanced around before wrapping several pastries with a couple of napkins and hiding them in his cargo pants. He couldn't be sure when he'd get a chance to eat again.

He followed Melon through a heavy glass door into what looked like a changing room. Lockers stood along one wall, and a second door opened to a room that was empty except for three long stainless steel tables. Melon flipped a switch that illuminated several banks of lights above them.

Melon looked around the room, pointing his finger in different directions as though mentally arranging it. He looked back at Kelly, smiled, and said, "Sorry, I'm just deciding where to put everything in our new procedure room."

"Procedure room?" Kelly asked.

"Never mind. Let's get all the boxes marked 'PR' into here. We can unpack them later."

They busied themselves carrying and dragging boxes into the room. Kelly wondered if they were ever going to get to all the boxes, and he began to slow as morning moved toward lunch. Just as he thought he couldn't lift another box, Melon stopped, looked at his watch, and said, "Let's get some lunch."

Kelly's hunger fought against his fear of being discovered, but he had little choice. He almost ran into Melon when the little man stopped abruptly. A tall man blocked their way. After surveying the room, he frowned at Melon but ignored Kelly and said, "So you're finally making some progress in here."

Melon stiffened and his voice quivered. "Yes, the supplies have finally arrived." He swallowed before continuing. "Kelly here is helping me unpack."

The man's face hardened as he looked around. He nodded, looked right through them, and left.

Melon pulled out a handkerchief and wiped his face with shaking hands.

"Who was that?" Kelly asked.

"That's Bauer. The less you have to do with him, the better off you'll be, believe me," Melon answered in a strained whisper.

"Is he in charge?" Kelly asked.

"No, Vandusen is—and trust me, you don't want to meet him either." Melon's voice quivered. He paused, looking at Kelly as though he wanted to elaborate, but only said, "Come on. Let's go to the mess hall before it closes."

His hunger winning out over his fear, Kelly followed Melon out the door.

Chapter Twenty-One

Tamara glanced into the rearview mirror as she turned onto Holcomb Lane and smiled when none of the traffic on Virginia Avenue turned to follow her. She breathed in the fragrant smells of the horse pastures, enjoying especially the fresh-cut alfalfa. In spite of her concerns, she stretched and relaxed a little. The whine of her VW Bug echoed off a corrugated hay barn. Usually, she would've put the top down and enjoyed the ride, but somehow it didn't feel right, even though these grassy pastures always made her homesick for Sweden. She downshifted as she turned onto the gravel drive of the chimp facility. A young man, probably a research grad student, waved her in. *Good, at least I'm expected.*

She slowed so as not to disturb two young trainers about her age who were walking a large chimp. Suddenly, the chimp ran toward her. She braked but relaxed when the chimp stopped short, held back by a long, taut leash, and held its hand out to her. She waved and drove on.

Her thoughts returned to what had happened to make her leave so abruptly from her office. She'd always felt isolated but safe down in the catacombs, as they were called, but she wondered who'd rung the buzzer and scared her enough to make her run out the fire exit like a common book thief.

At least the fire alarm would've brought security to check things out.

She parked when she saw Mary step out of the house and wave her in. Tamara grabbed the folder containing her research and followed the older woman inside.

Mary looked around before closing the door behind them. "Well, I see you're no worse for wear. Let me have a look at you. You're gorgeous!"

Tamara smiled and pulled her blond hair back, revealing her blue eyes. She started to reply but felt herself blushing and looked down at the floor instead.

"Don't be shy, dear. I should put you in one of my music videos. Really."

"I don't have any talent for getting in front of a camera."

"Trust me, with your looks, you don't need any. It's Hollywood." Mary led her into the dining room and motioned her to take a seat at the oak table, then she sat beside her. "So what is it you wanted to talk about?" she whispered with a frown.

Tamara fanned her folders out on the table where they could take advantage of the sunlight streaming through the bay window. The mood grew somber as Mary read through the clippings and notes. Tamara remembered her last visit and noticed that the kitchen was finally finished.

How different from my last visit.

Grunts came from the chimps outside, and finally, Mary looked up. Smiling, she said, "Food grunts. It's feeding time. Maybe we should take a hint and take a break."

Suddenly, Tamara felt starved. She nodded.

***

Tamara smacked her lips lightly and pushed her empty plate away. Only a trace of the enchiladas that Consuelo had prepared was left. Mary busied herself in the adjacent living room, lighting several faux bois floor lamps, probably left over from the old dude ranch days. Meanwhile, Consuelo carefully stacked the Wedgwood china and carried it through the swinging doors to the kitchen.

Tamara had felt uncomfortable, at first, when she learned Mary had invited Consuelo. She remembered the cold looks the woman had given her on her last visit. Perhaps Mary had talked with this fiery Mexican, because now she almost seemed friendly.

Mary smiled as though reading Tamara's mind. "Well, down to business. The boys have left for a recce into the woods."

Consuelo and Tamara looked at each other, confused.

"Excuse my English—what's a recce?" Tamara asked.

"Sorry, that's movie talk. The boys are doing a short recon up where they think Bigfoot or the creatures might be."

Tamara nodded. "That's why I wanted to get this information to them as soon as possible." She pulled out the Polaroid photo she'd taken of the map. "Take a look at this." Mary and Consuelo leaned in for a closer look.

"What is this?" Mary asked.

"Those pins represent the sightings over the last several years of Bigfoot in the general area of Willow Creek. Notice this dense cluster."

Consuelo interrupted. "Ken and the boys, as Mary calls them, are up in the Willow Creek area now. Lieutenant Sandy's coming down to fill us in on what they're up to."

Tamara nodded. She assumed they didn't want to use the phone for the same reason Mary hadn't. "If we look at the dates of these sightings, it appears the very early historic sightings and the more recent ones are clustered around this one area." She pointed at an arrow she'd drawn on the photo. "And all the other sightings radiate out chronologically from it."

The women nodded and looked at each other.

Mary picked up the photo for a closer look. "So what are you saying, exactly?"

"I think this one area is very important to whatever is out there." Tamara pulled out a geological map and pointed at a red circle she'd made. "This symbol, if you look at the legend, stands for a system of caves."

"There were—are—caves in Africa where the creatures we found lived," Mary said, handing the photo to Consuelo.

"It's cold up there and just going to get colder. Winter is coming," Consuelo said as she laid the photo down. "Those creatures, if there are any up there, would look for just such a place."

"True." Mary stood, left the room, and returned with a cart of desserts and coffee. An aroma of chicory filled the room. She beckoned them to partake.

Tamara helped herself to coffee and took a sip before saying, "The area around Willow Creek is surrounded by hundreds of miles of wilderness, and there've been a lot of sightings over the years. These caves seem to be the only ones of any magnitude in that whole area. But, as you can see from this map, it is very remote. It would a be long shot for them to find these or any other caves."

Consuelo nodded. "At least, not without help."

"What are you suggesting?" Mary asked.

"If there is such a thing as Bigfoot, and if it lives up there, caves would protect them from the cold."

"So you believe in these things?" Mary asked, smiling.

"You might change your mind when you go up there."

"So go up there and find where your husband and company have gotten to and help them find these caves," Tamara said.

"I think we should bring Chris and Sandy, if we're going up there," Mary said.

"Sandy? Isn't he up there with Ken already?" Consuelo asked.

Mary shook her head. "He was, but he came back to check in at his office and give us and Chris an update. I'm meeting him at the airport tomorrow."

Consuelo frowned. "Why didn't Ken just call?"

Mary looked at her. "Do you trust that Vandusen doesn't have someone listening in?"

"Ah. Good point."

Tamara nodded. "Someone rang my buzzer before I came here. It might seem silly, but I had a bad feeling. The library was closed, and no one should've had access. And worse, I thought I heard someone on the line when I was talking to you, Mary."

Mary tapped her knuckles on the table. "There you go. And Ken and I have the same feeling. Leave it to me to call Chris."

"But—"

"No worries, Tamara. As they say in show business, 'a nod is as good as a wink to a blind man.'" Mary smiled and tapped her nose.

Tamara frowned. "What does that mean?"

"It means," Consuelo said, "that Mary and Chris both speak movie lingo."

"And Vandusen's crew don't?"

Mary grinned. "Exactly."

Evening had set in, and the lamps struggled to light the room. They sat deep in their thoughts as Mary, the list-maker, began making a list. She finally put her pad down, smiled at them both, and said, "I think it's time to switch from coffee to something harder."

Their laughter filled the room.

Mary opened a cabinet containing an assortment of bottles and asked, "Should we visit Scotland or Ireland?" She reached for a bottle of Jameson and the others nodded in approval. Mary, officiating as the barmaid, poured their whiskey neat and handed out the glasses. They sat quietly for a while, sipping their drinks.

Mary broke the silence, saying, "Do you think this drama will ever end?"

"I . . . I don't think so," Consuelo replied and threw back her glass in one gulp.

Chapter Twenty-Two

The medic stood in the prep room, scrubbing for a second time. He couldn't stop his hands from shaking. Two of the remaining women they'd rescued from the caves had died before they could get everything ready to do this procedure. He figured that the embryos grew too large in the womb to be delivered naturally. The women's deaths had been horrific—medieval— and neither the infant nor the mother had survived. It had been unfortunate that all the physicians had left after they'd closed their old compound. According to François, he—a simple medic—was the most "qualified" medical professional left. They were frantically trying to get more qualified professionals back, but it was going to take time—time they didn't have. It was now or never for the last survivors, and worse, it was up to him.

He tore open the Betadine surgical scrub package and began scrubbing his fingernails with the coarse side. He used his knee to activate the lever for the hot water below the stainless steel sink and began the methodological procedure of scrubbing his hands and arms with the other side. After rinsing, he waited for everything to dry, holding his arms up and elbows away from anything that might not be sterile. The water slowly dripped from his elbows as he waited for everything to dry.

He mentally ran over every step again to be sure. He knew, of course, what he was doing now was the most important step: make sure everything was sterile. He'd practiced this process many times. It was especially important in the tropics. A patient was more likely to die from infection down here near the equator than any other complication from what he was about to do. His next step would be to enter the clean room they'd built. It was hardly a real operating room, but it was the closest thing to a sterile room they'd been able to design and build with what they had. It was probably the cleanest room within a five hundred-mile radius.

He felt a finality when he closed the door behind him. Two nurses greeted him with a nod and helped him with his surgical scrubs, cap, and mask. Thank god for them, the only professionals in the group who'd ever assisted with this procedure. He waited as one of the women adjusted his eye protection. They seemed to go through the motions of prepping with a business-as-usual calmness. If he could only get some of that. Finally, they both busied themselves helping him with his surgical gloves and shoes.

He'd assisted surgeons countless times in his life but only as an assistant and never on a procedure like this. Hell, he'd worked in more field hospitals than he could remember, all over the world, in countless war zones, while serving in the French Foreign Legion. He knew all about combat wounds and tropical illness, but this was a whole different business. His heart pounded so hard he thought it was going to fly out of his chest. He was already sweating so much that one of the women stopped him and wiped what was still exposed of his brow. He could barely speak.

There would be no backing out now. People had risked

their lives to procure the items he'd requested to perform this procedure. He needed to quit calling it a procedure and use its name: a cesarean section or C-section. It wasn't a procedure. That didn't get to the matter. It was a goddamn operation. His mouth was so dry he couldn't move his tongue when he tried to ask for a sip of water. He looked through the window that gave a view into the operating room and saw François standing there, pinning his loose sleeve. He considered asking someone to cover the window so no one could watch, but realized he had to act confident—like he knew what the hell he was doing.

My god, what have I gotten myself into? I'm going to kill this poor girl, for sure. He forced himself to change his train of thought back to the business at hand. She would die anyway if he didn't at least try to save her. A pretty little girl from one of a local tribes, probably not much older than fourteen, her abdomen had distended in a grotesque, deformed manner. She'd unexpectedly gone into labor early, and her contractions seemed so violent that they thought what was inside her womb would tear her apart. It sickened everyone attending to her. Her screams had been deafening, bringing horror to what should have been a joyful event. *It's ungodly.*

His surgical boots swished as he crossed the room. The nurses had done their job well, partially covering the patient with surgical wraps, and they'd neatly laid out all the instruments in the order he'd requested. *They know their job better than I do.*

A tap on the window startled him. It was that damn Belgian, François, giving him a thumbs-up. He frowned and tried to ignore him as he leaned over the table and looked down on the woman. She was out and looked like she was at least at peace—sleeping. He hoped she would stay that way and not be conscious to experience his butchering. No. He needed to stop thinking like that.

The whiff of ether made him dizzy, and he whispered, "Be careful with that valve, or you'll put us all under."

A nurse nodded and quickly checked the tank. He could hear the steady beeps of the heart monitor and the rhythmic breathing of the patient. He couldn't remember what either instrument was actually called just now, but it didn't matter. He realized he was stalling. It was time. He looked around at everyone in the OR and said, "Ready?"

The two nurses nodded. A man he didn't recognize, who sat by the monitors, cleared his throat before saying, "Yes, Doctor."

Doctor? If he only knew. But something in the man's voice reassured him. He held out his hand and ordered, "Scalpel."

This first incision had to be carefully executed so as not to go too deep and penetrate the uterus. He surprised himself when he realized his shakes had subsided. He leaned down, made the first incision, and opened the abdomen, then waited for the nurses to apply suction and retract enough for him to make the second incision into the uterus. He had to use even more care not to go too deep and harm the baby, just deep enough to rupture the amniotic sac surrounding it. He was so intent on his work, he didn't notice if the infant was alive or dead as a nurse helped him remove the baby from the uterus. He smiled when he felt it squirming. Another nurse quickly reached over and cut the umbilical cord as he carefully removed the placenta. Suddenly, the infant's cries filled the room. A nurse began cleaning the mother and child. The medic focused on cleaning the cavity and checking for injuries. Satisfied, he began suturing, first the uterus and then the abdomen. The worst was over. He felt dizzy. He needed to concentrate.

For the first time, the medic took notice of the infant. It looked human, and it was a boy. He smiled when he realized that the mother was breathing. They were both alive. But for how long? A wave of nausea passed over him, and he felt weak. He needed to get outside, feel the sunlight, and breathe fresh air. He struggled through the crowd who'd gathered outside the room, almost knocking over a startled soldier, and managed to pull off his hat and gown. He tried to steady himself against the porch railing, but the world spun and raced away from him, and then everything went dark.

***

The medic tried to focus on the blurry faces floating above him. The inside of his nose felt like it was fizzing with bubbles. Light was returning to the darkness. Someone had given him a dose of amyl nitrate. He coughed and tried to rise but felt an arm pushing him back down. He struggled but was too weak to get his way.

"Hold on, Doctor. You fainted and were out a long time. We were beginning to worry."

The medic recognized the voice of the man who'd assisted him in the operating room and whispered, "I'm not a doctor. Now let me sit up, goddamnit." He steadied himself with both hands as he sat and looked around at several people who stood there smiling at him.

"You did it, Doc," one of the nurses said while patting him on the arm. "It's nothing short of a miracle!"

Everything came back to him in a series of vivid flashes: the incisions, the sponging and suctioning, the crying infant, the suturing, and . . . So he'd actually pulled it off. He heard footsteps echoing across the room. *Where am I?* Blinding lights made it hard to see down a long hallway. François approached, his usually neatly tucked-in sleeve dangling.

Before the Belgian could say anything, the medic asked,

"How are the patients doing?"

"Your people are watching them closely, Doc. They seem to be recovering slowly, but they're alive." François kneeled beside him with a smile. "What are your post-op orders?"

The medic had to think back to what he'd read in the medical library, what seemed ages ago. He felt light-headed and fuzzy and was having trouble thinking clearly, but he finally gathered his thoughts and said, "We need to keep both infant and mom under close observation in the infirmary for at least two days. It's important to limit visits to just essential staff. Infection is our biggest concern, but the mom was healthy enough going into this. I'd say we should keep her on antibiotics and on fluids until tomorrow morning or so. Let's see how she and the baby do together. I'd rather not separate them."

"You're the doctor," François said. He started to stand but hesitated before continuing, "I'm more concerned about the infant. Several of the scientists are asking if you think he'll make it. You saw him. He looks pretty normal, except for the hair. This could be a real break for us."

"Will someone listen to me?" he yelled. "I'm not a doctor! I'm just a field medic. Hell, your guess is as good as mine."

"You're a doctor to us, Doc," a nurse whispered as she leaned over and kissed him on the cheek.

"Could you help me up?" the medic asked as he struggled onto one knee.

Another nurse raced over to help and he wobbled to his feet with both their help. A wave of nausea passed over him. The world had stopped spinning, but he still felt weak, like he'd gone ten rounds with Cassius Clay. However, his head cleared with each step as he made his way toward the infirmary with the help of the two nurses. At his urging the women reluctantly released his arms, and he was finally able to balance on his own.

His heart pounded when he pushed open the double doors. *What will I see?* The ward consisted of a row of empty beds, except the one at the far end by the window which framed the green tree line of the jungle. In that last bed, he could just make out the young woman holding her infant. The strong odor of Betadine assaulted him as he drew near them. The mother was conscious. She reached out to him, her hand trembling, and struggled to whisper, "*Asante sana.*"

"*Karibu* . . . You're welcome," the medic replied softly and arranged her linens.

She smiled weakly, closed her eyes, and hugged her baby close. Her breathing was shallow but steady.

The medic picked up a clipboard hanging on the metal frame of her hospital bed and reviewed her chart. All seemed in order. No fever, and her pain seemed under control—something very important for her recovery. He stared in wonder at the young woman holding her baby. The baby, except for a little more hair than he thought normal, looked to be wholly human. Even his cries seemed to be that of a human. He marveled that the mother was bonding so closely with the baby. Hard to understand, considering the events surrounding her pregnancy. *What strange magic is happening here? Could this be the bond of mother and a child no matter what the circumstances? How will this develop over time?*

Complications down the road were likely if this infant lived. The scientists would want to get their hands on him immediately. But he wasn't going to think about that just now. He stepped back as the nurses moved in and sponged the mother and infant. They busied themselves checking the young girl's dressings while rearranging her sheets. He admired their balance of tenderness and professional efficiency. One of the nurses bent over to lift the baby for a closer examination but let go when the mother moaned and pulled her back. The other nurse showed the mother the stethoscope she had hanging from her neck and mimed that she wanted to listen to her baby's heart. The mother weakly nodded and let her hold her baby.

The medic realized that it would be the nurses and their trained ability that would be most responsible for the outcome of this young girl and her baby. He was more in the way now. He wiped his brow with the back of his hand. The room fans above did little to relieve the heat and humidity. He needed to rest before he thought any more about all of this. He hung the clipboard with a clang that startled him and turned to leave. At the doors, he stopped and looked back, wondering if his patients would even be alive when he returned. Only time would tell. He headed for his quarters, knowing they would be in good hands—better than his own, in fact. The nurses knew their business and seemed to care, and caring was everything. He frowned, realizing he was looping. He just needed to close his eyes for a little while. It had been a long day.

Chapter Twenty-Three

Lester relaxed when he and Dusty finally pulled into Split Pea Anderson's gravel overflow parking lot. It had been a tense drive up the 101 after they dispatched the gunmen at the roadside. They'd tried to put some miles down the road, but Lester couldn't stop wondering what would've happened if Girlie hadn't been so quick to act. He hadn't seen her move that fast for years. She slept in her sleeping box now, immune to the swaying and bouncing of the Willys. Dusty seemed to be able to find every pothole on the decaying highway. Only a chimp could've fought for her life and then sleep like she hadn't a care in the world. Lester reached back and scratched her through the wire of her cage.

They'd sorted through the thugs' wallets while the men were unconscious but found no ID. Dusty had tried to blow the whole thing off as some crooks trying to make a score, but Lester knew better. This was Vandusen and his gangsters' work. *Dusty should know better. Hell, he was with us in Germany.*

Dusty slammed the door shut, jarring Lester out of his thoughts. He stepped out, feeling stiff and aching all over, and bent over to stretch his back. Rust fell from his hair. He brushed more out, looked at the rusting ceiling, and whispered,

"Piece of shit."

Lester tried to keep up with Dusty's pace as he walked toward the main entrance, but it was no use. Obviously, Dusty was hell-bent on getting some food in his gut. Lester slowed. The parking area wasn't lit, and gopher holes peppered the ground. He paused to catch his breath and took in the restaurant and adjacent hotel. The Nordic architecture complete with windmills set in the Central Coast with its rolling hills, oaks, grapevines, and wooden barns had always seemed out of place. But he was relieved, just the same, to stop somewhere familiar and crowded. He'd have a chance to talk to Dusty about what he thought they should do with Oliver and Danny when they got to Reno, but first he'd call Mary and let her know they were on their way.

***

"You want to do what? What happened to just going up to Reno, helping Mary with the compound, and being ready to move Oliver and Danny if and when the time came?" Dusty asked as he looked up from the menu.

"I gather from what Mary said that they're being watched, and she thinks we should move Oliver and Danny when we get there. They're not safe there anymore. She didn't mention them by name, but I knew who she meant. It's all very mysterious." Lester kept his voice low, though there was little chance of them being overheard in a restaurant overflowing with tourists.

"Who's 'they'?" Dusty asked as he laid down his menu and motioned to a passing waitress.

Lester waited until the waitress left with their orders before answering, "Mary, Consuelo, and Tamara. Ken and the rest have left for Willow Creek, which leaves Mary trying to keep an eye on things in Reno."

"So you think what just happened down the road is connected to us going up to Reno?"

Lester shrugged. "Whoever's watching them could be watching us as well." He waited for that to sink in before continuing. "Of course, Ken and Fred's students are there, but they'd be way over their heads dealing with Oliver and Danny."

Dusty frowned.

"But as far as what I think we should do with them—let's wait until you have a full stomach before we talk more on that." Lester smiled at the plump waitress as she slid two steaming bowls of split pea soup in front of them.

Dusty grinned as he stuffed a paper napkin in the neckline of his T-shirt and fanned it ever so delicately. "Now you're talking."

They busied themselves with their dinner, though Lester couldn't help but keep looking at the reception area and watch the comings and goings. When he spied two sheriffs weaving their way through the crowd of patrons waiting to be seated and making a direct path toward what looked to be a manager, Lester set his spoon down and tapped Dusty. "That doesn't look good. I think they're looking for someone."

Dusty looked up, then nudged Lester to slide out of the booth.

Lester led the way, this time. While the sheriffs spoke to the manager, they slipped outside and faded into the shadows, heading back toward their wagon. When he looked back over his shoulder, Lester noticed the sheriffs making their rounds between the parked cars near the restaurant's front entrance. "I think we need to put some miles down the road," he said as they climbed into the Willys.

Dusty pulled the choke several times and cranked the engine.

Lester leaned over the dash, wiped the dust and rust off the radio, and turned it on. At first, as he turned the tuner, he only heard static. Finally, he settled on the only station that seemed to come in clear and turned to calm Girlie as they bumped across the field before reaching the highway. Since Girlie was awake now, Lester let her out of her sleeping box and offered her the sandwich he'd bought for her, but she didn't take it. Instead, she turned and raced to the back window.

"What are you looking for, Girlie?" he asked in a strained voice. "Come and get your sandwich."

Girlie ignored him and continued to watch out the back window.

"And where do you suggest we take them?" Dusty finally asked.

As though timed, "Ventura Highway" by America broke clear of the static as Dusty accelerated north on the 101. Lester smiled and whispered, as though to himself, "Fitting. The road knows." He punched Dusty on the shoulder. "We've spent our lives on the road. The safest place for us is to get back on it. We know it and can keep Oliver and Danny safe as long as we stay on it and keep moving. That'll buy Ken some time. What say we head up their way?"

Dusty gazed at Lester for several heartbeats before nodding.

Chapter Twenty-Four

Dr. Melon swore to himself as he surveyed their progress. The observation room they'd built was cold and damp but at least quiet from the loud cries of the hybrids. They'd built a large soundproof wall to separate where he and Vandusen stood from the caged creatures on the other side. They could watch them from a large black-and-white monitor that hung from the ceiling. Bauer's men had built the lab inside an old Quonset hut left over from when this place had been a logging camp. He could almost feel Vandusen's eyes drilling into him. He needed time to think, but Vandusen was getting impatient, and he'd seen with his own eyes what that could mean.

He took a deep breath and tried to pick his words carefully. "I don't think they're ever going to breed as long as we have them caged. Everything is wrong. We can't duplicate the proper conditions for the hybrids up here. They've lived their whole lives free and in the wilds of Africa. Our very presence sets them off, besides the cold and dampness." His lips quivered as he watched this sink into Vandusen's thick skull.

"So you're telling me that after all this money and work, you can't produce a single offspring from these freaks?" Vandusen's voice grew louder. "You're the one who told me that we needed to breed these freaks so we could separate the offspring and start training them when they were young and manageable. You better think of something quick. The general will be back sooner than you'd like. If you don't produce results, he'll have us flatten your little pinhead."

Melon looked out the window. The trees surrounding the old logging camp were damp, and a mist had settled in the clearings, but the compound was clean and organized and, more importantly, finished. Vandusen and his men, especially Bauer, had been busy. They'd gotten the workmen to produce more in a month than he'd been able to do in six.

Vandusen started to walk out but turned at the door. His face hardened when he said, "I've got an idea. How about we throw that precious little daughter of yours into one of those cages? That might wake those freaks of nature up, or at the very least, it would give us some sport in this soggy shithole."

Despite the cold dampness of the room, Melon felt a chill sweep over him. For several heartbeats, he couldn't make his mouth move.

Vandusen smirked with amusement as his cold, black eyes watched that sink in.

Melon finally spoke. "I have an idea. We can try in vitro fertilization."

Vandusen glared and asked, "What the fuck is that?"

Melon struggled to simplify a complex procedure for this simpleton to understand. "It's an important step in artificial insemination for humans. Only, here we can try it on the hybrids. We take the sperm of a male and insert it—"

"Wait." Vandusen walked back into the lab, pulled up a chair, and motioned Melon to sit.

Melon knew that Vandusen was also worried that the general might show up and he'd have no results to show him. Melon had listened to Vandusen stretch the truth during his phone conversations with the general.

"I don't give a shit how it works, as long as it works," Vandusen said. "What kind of equipment do we need? And how long will it take to get it happening?"

Melon told him what he could, but without consulting a book, his explanation came out vague and rambling.

Vandusen cut him off. "Never mind that. How much will it cost?"

Melon wrung his hands before answering. "A lot . . ." Seeing Vandusen's brow furrow, he quickly added, "But this will work. I'm sure of it." Right now Melon would promise anything to keep his family safe.

"You better be sure, or I'll throw the whole lot of you in to play with these monsters. Make me a list." Vandusen looked at Melon in disgust and left.

Melon realized he was running out of time.

***

The rainy season had arrived, and it was raining again. Melon cursed this godforsaken place as he tried to balance on the planks the workmen had placed to span the mud puddles. He hated it here. It seemed it was always raining in this cold, damp hollow. The mist swirled like fog and dripped off every overhang. He swore when he slipped off the soggy walkway and stepped into ankle-deep mud. He swore again when the suction pulled his shoe off, and he watched helplessly as it filled and disappeared into the puddle. Several men laughed as they watched him try to retrieve his shoe while waving his shoeless foot in the air. Just as he was about to follow his shoe into the mud, he felt someone grab his arm and steady him.

"Thank you. I'm not doing too well here."

A young man smiled back at him and said, "I'd say that's an understatement." While holding Melon, the man leaned over and retrieved the shoe. "Here you go." Before Melon could say anything, the man continued, "I'd say you're having more problems than just trying to cross this muddy compound."

Melon thought he recognized this young man. Looking him up and down, he said, "You're the young man who was so helpful setting up the procedure room."

"That's right. How's everything going up there?" His new friend pointed to where they'd worked together.

Just then, out of the corner of his eye, Melon caught Bauer watching them from one of the guard shacks. He hastily pulled on his shoe and said, "Again, thank you. You've been most kind."

The young man glanced sidelong in Bauer's direction and said, "No worries. We'll talk again." He made a quick path along the boards, skipping puddles as best he could, and faded into the mist.

Melon hurried, picking his way toward his house and family.

Who is this young man who keeps popping up? He'd been the only person to show him any kindness since he'd been kidnapped and whisked away to this miserable nightmare. He was sure he wasn't part of Vandusen's gang, but he couldn't figure out what he was doing in their midst. He could make out the lights of his home away from home now and hurried to get out of the rain, but not before looking back in the direction in which the young man had gone. He only saw the swirls of windblown rain. The compound flashed with lightning, followed by claps of thunder as the storm freshened. He'd have to think about this later.

Chapter Twenty-Five

The Ohmah rarely came down to where the humans dwelled anymore. But the leader had to see this new village the humans were building near where they picked blackberries. He scratched his matted amber hair and looked over his shoulder, surprised to find he was alone. Where had the rest of his band gone? The lights shining from the clearing below blinded him. He preferred scouting in the dark, especially when the Maiden was behind the clouds. Her silver glow often lit his way in the darkness, but tonight he would have to hide in the night shadows. The Maiden was a friend of the Ohmah.

He could feel dark magic adrift in the forest. It came from these new arrivals that he and his kin had stumbled across. And worse, a new settlement of humans grew where the old logging camp had once been. Evil had come to visit them, and he would have to stop it. These new creatures had caused the humans to be afoot in his homeland, and worse, they were bringing attention to their way of life. These black creatures had raided a campground in the foothills not long ago. They had broken the rule of the Maiden to not harm the humans.

He was the leader and would have to do something soon, but he wasn't sure what. They had found the scattered wreckage of the big silver bird and had followed for many miles tracks that plowed through the woods. Their best trackers didn't recognize what had made them, and that had confused them, but now they knew. They'd lost the trail in the rocky ridges, but later, while crossing the river at the bridge the humans had built, they'd discovered who'd made these tracks. They'd come close to a battle, but everything had changed when one of the females of his kin had fallen into the river. A big, black creature, maybe their leader, had pulled her out, so he had let the newcomers pass. He didn't understand why he had but thought it might be the work of the Maiden. He would have to wait.

He tried to count the humans below but ran out of numbers. There were many, too many, and they had weapons that shot fire and killed at a distance. He didn't like it. Worse, he could hear strange cries from the buildings inside the fence. He thought they sounded like the cries these new creatures made. This worried him. These creatures were noisy and would bring attention to his band if they didn't learn to live and stalk silently.

He and his kin had lived quietly since the Fathers had come across the ice. They'd left the humans alone, and the humans had done the same, most of the time. The forest was the Ohmah's home. They stayed away from the human villages and lived secretly. All this pleased the Maiden. But these new arrivals had brought evil to the forest and broken the rules. They—he— would have to do something. He would go to the sacred caves and pray to the Maiden before these newcomers spilled more blood. She would know what to do.

He turned and faded into the darkness as silently as he had come.

Chapter Twenty-Six

Lt. Sandy walked down the steps to the tarmac below. Mary stood with Consuelo and Tamara near the luggage area. He waved, and she smiled and motioned him over.

"Lieutenant Sandy!" a familiar voice called from behind him.

He turned to see Dr. Chris Raven jogging across the tarmac toward him. He must have just arrived on another flight.

"I didn't expect to see you again so soon," Sandy said.

"Mary called just after you left. She wants to head up to Willow Creek and wanted me to go with her. I gather she has something Ken needs to see."

"Hmm. Must be important."

Chris nodded, and as they made their way across the runway, he asked, "Who's that blonde with Mary and Consuelo?" Chris didn't like surprises, not even tall, slender ones, not when it came to this business with Vandusen and his cronies.

"It's okay," Sandy replied. "She's the expert librarian who's been helping Ken and Fred." He quickened his pace.

"Oh, the one who helped with the photos Bobby found in Mexico?"

Sandy nodded. "They say she's even smarter than she is beautiful. I love her accent."

"Accent?"

"Yep. She's Danish, I think."

"How were things at the office?" Chris asked.

"Let's just say, I'm glad I went."

Mary hugged Sandy and smiled at Chris before whispering, "Let's get your bags and get out of here." She cast a furtive glance around them, then headed toward the luggage area but paused on the other side of the glass doors and said, "Wait. I forgot the introductions. You all know Consuelo, and this young lady is Tamara. She's been helping us on this . . . this project."

Chris met Tamara's striking blue eyes, momentarily at a loss for words.

She smiled and held out her hand. "It's a pleasure, Dr. Raven. Fred and Ken speak highly of you."

Chris noticed that she looked down when she mentioned Fred's name. He smiled to himself. *Fred can be as bad as Mark when it comes to gorgeous women.* When he realized everyone was waiting for him to say something, he said, "I . . . I think we should mount up and get rolling."

"Exactly my thoughts as well," Mary said. "My Mercedes is in the parking lot. I'll fetch it." She raced off ahead of them, then looked back over her shoulder and mouthed, "I'll pick you up out front."

Chris nodded, and he and Sandy tailed Consuelo and Tamara. They had difficulty weaving their way through the crowd pushing and bumping to catch their flights. This sleepy little airport in Reno had undergone a metamorphosis. The inside had been remodeled into a modern decor of glass, chrome, and Formica. The new carpet even still smelled of glue. It was an international airport now. Lines of passengers filled the boarding areas, waiting to fly to almost any location in the world—a perfect place to blend in, if they didn't stay too long, and it seemed that was Mary's plan. The women led the way to the luggage carousels.

Consuelo turned to Sandy and said in an all-business tone, "Here, give me your luggage tickets." She handed the checker the tickets and nodded back at Chris and Sandy.

Chris noticed that after the man looked them up and down and waved them through, he picked up a telephone. He couldn't hear him, but he could see him speaking, and the man kept watching them. *Not very subtle.* Chris didn't understand why the avocado color of the phone put him off so much, but it did, in spite of his worries. *I must be losing it. I need to get a grip.*

Tamara closed in next to him and whispered, "So you noticed that too?"

Chris could just see through the glass doors that the man was still looking in their direction, phone to his ear. He'd been so intent on watching him that he hadn't noticed they'd reached the sidewalk of the passenger-loading area. A police officer, busy directing a stream of traffic, wasn't letting anyone stop in the loading area. Chris looked back again. Two men stood at the checkout counter now, talking to the man as he hung up the phone, and all three looked at Chris.

Tamara was watching the men as well. She pulled his arm and motioned him to follow her.

When they joined Consuelo and Sandy, Chris said to Tamara, "I'm sorry, you asked me something, didn't you?"

She winked and said, "I think you've already answered me."

Consuelo and Sandy were in deep conversation and hadn't noticed that the men had left the counter and were making their way toward them. Luckily, a tour group following a woman holding an umbrella up and yelling "My tour, my tour!" got in their way.

A car drew up beside them with a squeal of brakes. Chris

jumped, but it was only Mary. She'd pulled into the closed loading area despite the officer ordering her to move on. She just smiled as they jumped in and slammed the doors. The officer pounded on her hood and pointed to indicate she should join the steady flow of traffic. Mary tried to pull out, but only succeeded in inciting a symphony of horns.

The men who'd been watching them noticed the officer and stopped just outside the exit, watching the chaos. Just when Chris was sure they were going to be arrested, another officer arrived and stepped out into the lane to hold traffic so Mary could exit. Chris exhaled loudly as they entered the flow of airport madness. "So much for arriving and leaving incognito."

Mary laughed, throwing her amber hair back out of her face. "You saw those suits as well." Consuelo and Sandy turned and joined Chris and Tamara in looking back. The rear window framed the two men standing on the curb. They sighed in unison as the two men faded in the distance. Mary weaved through the stream of traffic with ease.

"What the hell was that all about?" Chris asked, leaning forward over the back seat.

Mary adjusted the rearview mirror so she could see in the back. "We've had a feeling someone's been following us since Tamara left the university yesterday."

"Who?"

"We're not sure, but Tamara had a scare yesterday—Oops!" Mary swerved back into her lane and, ignoring the honking, continued, "Someone buzzed her office when the library was closed."

"No one should've been inside," Tamara said with a strained voice, "but I can't be sure. It was just a feeling, and now these two men . . ." She bit her lip.

"I don't believe in coincidences," Sandy said.

Mary nodded. "Neither do I. Not since Ken got us all into this mess."

"Ken sent me back from Willow Creek to let you know they were going on a little hike into the wilderness with a Native American named, Jimmy Two-Feathers," Sandy said. "He's from the local Hupa tribe. He was going to take them up to some sacred rock paintings and guide them around the area where he claims to have seen Bigfoot."

"Why there?" Consuelo asked.

Sandy looked at Consuelo. "Vandusen might have brought some of the creatures from Africa back here and somehow lost them in that area. Ken thinks the creatures did that massacre and that recent sightings supposedly of Bigfoot might have been of escaped creatures. He's convinced that Bigfoot and the creatures are connected somehow."

Chris frowned. "Does Ken actually have evidence of any of this?"

"You know Ken. He wouldn't be up there unless he had something to go on," Mary said as she took the on-ramp for the I-80. She turned the headlights on as it was getting dark and continued, "I know he was very interested in the news that the DOD was opening a primate center where an old logging camp had been near Willow Creek."

"Yes," Sandy added. "He got really interested when he heard that Dr. Melon was rumored to be heading it up, but none of this is confirmed."

"Melon is up there? You're sure of that?" Chris asked, almost spitting out his words.

"We think he's up there," Mary said, "but no one has heard from him or his family since he supposedly took the position." She frowned. "It's said to be a top secret facility. Very convenient, don't you think?"

"Hmmm." Chris nodded. "Do we know anything about this facility?"

"I met a forest ranger named Kelly up there," Sandy said. "He was going to have a look around and see what he could find out about the place. He's been helping with the massacre investigation. The sheriff hired him as a tracker, so I guess he's pretty good. He's searching for those lost girls and who or what abducted them."

Tamara rummaged through a leather briefcase and said, "I have some data that may help with that. That's why I contacted Mary in the first place."

Mary looked over her shoulder. "There's a dome light above you."

Consuelo reached for the steering wheel and yelled, "Please keep your eyes on the road, Mary!"

Mary smiled and shrugged but returned her focus to negotiating her lane.

"Where are we headed, anyway?" Chris asked, realizing for the first time that they were headed west on the I-80, speeding in the opposite direction to Ken's facility.

"Willow Creek," Mary said. "Where else?"

Given what he'd just learned, that seemed to Chris like the logical move.

"Wait," Sandy said. "There's one other thing." He paused.

"What?" Mary asked.

"Is Lester here yet?"

"No, but they shouldn't be far away."

Sandy sighed. "Ken wants him to bring Oliver and Danny to Willow Creek. He doesn't think they're safe at the compound anymore."

"It's okay," Mary said. "Chris's trailer and transfer cages arrived, and the head trainer knows to help Lester get them on the road as soon as they get there."

"But Willow Creek?" Consuelo asked. "If Vandusen's there, won't they be in danger?"

"If creatures did that massacre," Sandy said quietly, "Oliver and Danny may be the key to bringing them in."

"Oh. Right." Consuelo fell into silence.

"I'll have to get gas soon," Mary said, "so I can call and leave a message for Lester with the head trainer."

"In code," Consuelo reminded her.

Mary chuckled. "Of course."

Tamara handed Chris an unfolded sheet. He held it up to the dome light to get a good look. "This is very interesting, Tamara. There's been a major uptick in sightings in the last six months in the woods surrounding Willow Creek. Very good work."

Tamara smiled. "Especially when you consider these incidents coincide with about the time that facility started construction. And that's about the time Dr. Melon dropped out of sight."

Chris nodded. "Vandusen and his cronies."

"Or worse . . ." Tamara whispered.

"Worse? What do you mean?" Sandy asked.

"What if there really are creatures loose in the woods and they've awakened something sleeping in there?" She peered into the darkness out the window.

"Bigfoot? Is that what you mean?" Chris said, trying not to smile.

Consuelo glared at him. "Before you laugh at the idea, you need to go up there and see for yourself."

Mary was amused that Consuelo, of all people, was taking Tamara's side. She thought back to the first time they'd been together in a room, and how uncomfortable Mark had been. She had to work not to laugh. That was funnier than the idea of Bigfoot being discussed by these eggheads.

"Sorry, I meant no offense," Chris said hastily. He looked around and saw they were all dead serious about bringing that hairy devil into the discussion.

"I forgot to tell you this back at your place," Sandy said, "but Kelly showed me a plaster cast he made just a few days ago of a huge humanoid footprint that could've been made by one of the creatures, if not a bigfoot."

Chris snorted. "Casts can easily be faked."

Sandy nodded. "True. Ken hasn't seen it yet, but Kelly has nothing to gain by declaring it Bigfoot. In fact, he's reticent to apply the term or let anyone know he has it. He's also heard cries that don't come from any animal he knows, and he explained why the print he took the cast from didn't look faked. He doesn't know what it is, but as he said to me, something's out there."

Chris frowned. He didn't think this was the time or the place to argue the Bigfoot issue. Surely when he met Ken and Fred, clearer heads would prevail.

"And then there's the plane wreckage, complete with broken cages," Sandy continued.

"What?" the girls said at once.

Sandy relayed what Kelly had told him, including the nonhuman hair samples he'd found.

"And Bigfoot or not, that supports the theory that Vandusen could have brought some of the creatures here and lost them," Chris said.

"When their plane crashed," Tamara said.

They became silent, deep in their own thoughts, until Mary startled them and asked, "Anyone hungry?"

Chapter Twenty-Seven

The general smiled as the driver made the turn through the open gates of his new compound. He saw Vandusen walking down the drive and tapped the driver on the shoulder. "I'll get out here. Let's stop by Mr. Vandusen."

The general couldn't believe his eyes as he surveyed the compound. "Hell, you've been busy!"

"Thank you, sir." Vandusen pointed up the hill toward Bauer who was supervising two men unloading two trucks next to a Quonset hut. "That building is where we'll be doing the observations for the crossbreeding."

"So this scientist will be able to pull this off? We're running out of time." The general covered his eyes against the sun and looked around. The tangled mess of the old logging camp was cleaned up. He cursed under his breath, thinking of the time wasted with that idiot Melon overseeing everything. He looked around again. The fencing was almost all up, and the piles of logs and debris had been burned or hauled away. It was beginning to look like something the DOD would be proud to call home. He thought of all the covert facilities he'd overseen being constructed on the many tours he'd served. This one was tricky, since it was in the States, which was always challenging. He preferred building them in the shitholes of the world where you could spread a little money around and renegade governments would fall in line. This place was perfect, secluded in the woods, and their cover as a US Army primate facility was perfect, but you still had to look out for some pain-in-the-ass sheriff—or worse, senator—to gum up the works. It might have been better to have stayed in the Congo, though that seemed to be a lost effort now, but time would tell. He was a patient man.

Vandusen looked at the general with concern. "Something wrong, sir?"

"Nothing we can't clear up as soon as you tell me when we don't need Melon anymore," the general said, smiling. He didn't like nonbelievers in their midst, even if they were under lock and key. He noticed that Vandusen looked confused and continued, "Not to worry. We'll keep him on as long as we need him. He's still a perfect front and has the knowledge we need. I'd rather not bring any more 'experts' into the fold. So we're stuck with the asshole, for now."

Vandusen nodded in agreement. "We still need him for a while longer. In fact, he's up stocking the new observation room right now. We hired some men from a town on the coast, Eureka, I think, to move this along."

"You agree? We still need him?" the general asked.

"A little while longer. I want him to set up the procedures we're going to need to get this breeding program going. I don't have a clue how to set that up. Hell, I thought we'd just throw a couple women in with those freaks and wait and see what we get. Melon insists that won't work, and he's the only expert we have." Vandusen lowered his voice to stay out of earshot from the driver.

The general's face twisted into a leer. "So do you have any volunteers, or do you need some help from our end? We have plenty of captives from Central America right now that should help you. In fact, it might help us in our interrogations if we had some video footage to show some of these Contras what's in store for them if they don't help us out with some intel."

Vandusen laughed. "We'll need lots of subjects once we get everything set up, sir. But first, I have one lined up from our end."

"Really? Who's that?"

Vandusen pointed at the house on the hill where Melon and his family were quartered. "They live up there."

The general thought a minute before nodding. "You mean from Melon's family?"

Vandusen grinned. "Yes, he has a pretty little teenage daughter and a wife who's not bad."

The two men laughed, and the driver looked around, puzzled.

"That's brilliant, young man, brilliant," the general whispered between laughs. He paused before continuing, "We'll leave the good professor intact for now, so he gets the opportunity of observing this experiment. We wouldn't want him to miss the rewards of all his hard work."

"Of course! And we have Mrs. Melon in the bullpen if our first try fails," Vandusen added.

They stood gazing at the house on the hill as the driver busied himself dusting off the suburban.

The general turned toward the driver, breaking the spell. "Let's go find the good professor. We have much to talk about."

The driver looked confused until Vandusen said, "He's up at that Quonset hut where they're unloading the trucks. We'll be able to catch up there."

Chapter Twenty-Eight

Kelly slipped behind a metal shed, setting off a chorus of unnerving cries. He peered around the corner just in time to spy several men armed with rifles headed in his direction. *Shit!* He was quickly running out of options. His chance was blown. Ever since he'd sneaked into the compound, he'd wanted to know what was making all the racket inside the building, but security had been tight day and night. This had been his first chance to even get near it. Time had run out, and now he needed to disappear. He turned, slinked into the swirling fog, and headed back toward the fence. He worried he wouldn't be able to find where he'd dug his way under. *How long had it been, two, three days?* It was hard to see in the dense fog, but at least it gave him cover.

His legs buckled as he stood near where he thought he'd crawled under the fence. His stomach growled, startling himself. He dug his hand into his cargo pants and chuffed the last crumbs of the donuts he had scavenged when helping that scientist. *Melon certainly didn't seem to fit in with this mob.* He'd located Lt. Sandy's missing person.

Muffled voices moved in his direction, and he sprang into action. Just when he thought he'd have to double back, he tripped over something—his pack. What a relief. He kneeled down and fumbled around in it for a moment until he found his pistol. The faint image of someone came toward him through the mist. He froze in place as they passed by so close, he could've reached out and touched them. After they'd gone, he pulled out his canteen and carefully unscrewed the cap, stopping after several twists to listen, then he downed what was left and crawled to the fence line. Fortunately, the cleanup crews hadn't reached this part of the grounds.

Searching in the darkness was like playing blindman's buff. He wasn't sure what he was bumping into, but after several false attempts, he found the hole he'd made under the fence. With everything cloaked under a blanket of fog and mist, he found it hard to follow the path he'd cleared, but he was careful not to stray off his previous trail, as he suspected the area was littered with mines. *Who are these people?*

Finally, Kelly reached the outer fence and could just make out the forest line looming up outside the clearing that surrounded the facility. He sensed it more than he saw it. He pushed his backpack ahead of him under the fence, then followed, crawling the rest of the way. Once hidden in the trees, he stood and brushed himself off. Suddenly he felt hungry. *Time to get out of here.*

He crept up the path he'd followed several days before and wondered again who'd made it. It was wider than a typical game trail. At a bend in the path, out of sight of the fence line, he dug deep in his pack and devoured the remaining granola bars and nuts.

Between mouthfuls, he listened, but he only heard the incessant cries that emitted from that mysterious building day and night. He swore under his breath, wishing he'd been able to find out what made those unearthly cries.

Yells suddenly rose up in the darkness, jarring him out of his musings, and several flashlight beams cut the night behind him. Apparently, his excavations had been discovered. It was time to fade into the forest and put this adventure behind him. He'd risked a lot, but it had paid off. He'd been lucky. It was time to contact Lt. Sandy. They had much to talk about.

Chapter Twenty-Nine

Mary stood blocking the doorway of the motel room with one foot pointing into the room. She made a sucking noise with the tip of her tongue against her teeth and shook her head. "Well, here we are."

Chris smiled and said, "It's not the Bonaventure, is it?"

"It will have to do," Mary said with a sigh.

When they'd settled into their respective rooms, they gathered in Mary's room to discuss their next move.

"Here," Sandy said. "Take a look at this." He handed Mary a note.

She took the note from Sandy. Her hands trembled as she read it. "Where did you get this?"

"Our contact with the ham radio operator in Hunt's old haunts in San Francisco sent it to Hunt," Sandy said as he parted the dusty paisley curtains. "Before Hunt left, he gave her my contact info. I picked it up when I checked in at my office before I flew to meet you. That woman has stayed in contact with François since we left. I guess Bobby paid her well."

Tamara and Consuelo closed in and tried to read the note over Mary's shoulder. Mary sighed and handed it to Consuelo before looking back at Sandy. "Well, it looks like they finally did it."

Sandy nodded. "Yes."

Mary could just see between the parted curtains of the window of the Bigfoot Motel out to the empty parking lot. Very little traffic passed on the highway that ran through town. A gust blew leaves across the asphalt. The town was empty since the media had lost interest and left for more dramatic news. Apparently, the local sheriff and the ranger they'd hired hadn't turned up much that would excite the reporters, so they'd left as quickly as they'd arrived. While it bothered Mary that the media could be so callous, it didn't surprise her. She knew that TV news was just another kind of show business. Ken had told her before he'd left with that local, Jimmy Two-Feathers, to be careful, because they'd stand out when the town emptied.

"It's a real breakthrough, right?" Sandy asked before he closed the curtains.

"That's a Ken question, but I'd say it is," Mary replied. "Of all things . . . Who would've thought?"

Sandy reread the note as the women looked at each other without a word.

Tamara broke the silence. "They've delivered a hybrid."

"No, a monster. A creature," Consuelo said. She walked across the dingy room and reached for a bottle of Patrón. Sandy and Tamara joined her at the sink. "So where do we go from here?" she asked.

"We need to contact Ken and the rest of the group. This is a game changer, I think," Mary said. "But where are they? I thought they'd be back by now."

"How about we pay a visit to the sheriff?" Chris suggested. "See what he knows."

Sandy shook his head. "Good luck with that. I'm waiting until Kelly gets back."

"How long does it take to scout out a place?" Chris asked.

Sandy sighed. He'd expected the man to have returned by now. "See if the sheriff has seen him. Perhaps he's back and just not near his phone."

***

The sheriff looked from Mary to Chris. Consuelo stood behind their chairs and frowned. He tapped his fingers on the desk and couldn't help but look at the closed door to his office every time someone passed. Where the hell was Sandy and Kelly? He hadn't seen either of them since they'd left his office.

They stood in silence, regarding each other, waiting for someone to speak. Mary jumped at the rattling of an AC vent when the air conditioner kicked in. "We thought we'd just check in and see if you'd seen or heard anything from my husband or anyone else in his group," she said. "I understand you met with Lt. Sandy a few days ago. He's working with my husband and his colleagues."

"Lt. Sandy did stop by here but only mentioned the rest of his group. I never met them. What are they working on, if I may ask?" The sheriff watched them closely. They seemed nervous to him, but he couldn't decide if they were just worried that they couldn't find their group, or if there was more to this call.

"My husband is researching Bigfoot, and Lt. Sandy is investigating a missing person, a Dr. Melon," Mary said.

"How did they find themselves working together?" the sheriff asked.

"I'm really not sure . . . I know he knew Dr. Melon, the missing person."

"We heard they were heading into the backcountry with a fellow called Jimmy Two-Feathers," Chris said, "but I would've thought they'd be back by now. Do you know this character? Is he trustworthy?"

"I know him," the sheriff replied. "He's a reliable fellow. He'll get them back safe and sound. There's no need to worry."

"Is there anyone you can send after them, just to make sure nothing's happened to them? What with that massacre and all . . ." Mary trailed off.

The sheriff sighed. "We're a small town, ma'am. I don't have men to spare to go tromping around out there looking for people who left with an experienced and reliable guide. Give it a couple more days, and we can look at the situation again."

"Have you noticed any other strangers in town, now that the festival is over?" Chris asked.

The sheriff frowned. "Not that I've noticed, but why would that be of concern to you?"

"Spies," Mary said quickly. She smiled sweetly. "People looking to filch my husband's research. Academia is highly competitive."

"I see. He carries his research with him, does he?" He was sure she winced just a little before she laughed his question off, likely to give her time to fabricate more lies.

"No, but it is well known in academic circles that he carries the key to a locker that houses his most sensitive work."

"Hmmm." The sheriff thought he should be getting used to these big-city visitors after all the press and media that had invaded them. He found it stressful walking the razor's edge of sharing too much or being branded uncooperative. But somehow, these people standing in front of him were different. They seemed to know a lot about what Sandy and Kelly were investigating. But how? Did they have something to do with the plane crash, or the massacre? "Are you just up here to locate your husband, or is there something else that's drawn your attention?"

he asked, looking at each member of the group in turn.

"Just wondering where he is," Mary said.

"I've heard whispers that a producer I often work with might be planning a movie with Bigfoot in it," Chris said. "In which case, he'd be looking to me for help furnishing an animal that might pass for one—at least, at a distance. Hence my interest in what Dr. Turner finds."

The sheriff was sure the man was lying, though he couldn't think why. He looked at Consuelo, but she said nothing, just kept frowning at him. He could tell he wasn't going to get much more with this line of questioning but decided to tell them some of what he knew—which wasn't much. "I haven't heard from either Detective Sandy or Ranger Kelly since they left my office a week ago. I encouraged them to work together. I think Kelly planned to search for your person of interest in the backcountry." He let that set in while he watched his visitors closely. Clearly, they were confused.

"Well, thank you, sir, for your assistance. I guess we'll just wait until we hear from them," Mary said as she gathered up her purse. "We'll be staying at the Bigfoot Motel. If you should hear from them first, I'd—we'd be most grateful if you contacted us."

The sheriff relaxed his jaw as he watched his visitors make a hasty retreat. He rubbed the side of his chin; his dentist had warned him that he was slowly grinding his teeth.

What the hell are they really up to? he wondered.

Chapter Thirty

Lester and Dusty could hear the cries as they drove up the drive of the Reno compound.

"What in the hell is going on? That's Oliver and Danny," Lester said, frowning.

"Goddamn freaks of nature." Dusty pulled up next to the Turners' residence.

A grad student raced up to them, gesturing them to stay in the vehicle. "Are you Lester and Dusty?"

"That's us," Dusty said.

"Mrs. Turner and the others have gone to Willow Creek to take some information to Dr. Turner. She said you need to move Danny and Oliver as soon as you get here." He pointed toward the barn at the end of the gravel drive. "They're trying to get them into transfer cages."

"They're trying to do what?" The student started to answer, but Lester ignored him. "Get this heap of shit over there, pronto," he said to Dusty. "That racket is coming out of the hay barn they converted to hide them."

Dusty pulled up outside the barn and Lester jumped out, followed by Girlie, and headed in the direction of the cries. He took her hand and led the way. Dusty lagged several paces behind, shaking his head and mumbling to himself.

Lester thought about his last conversation with Mary. She'd been relieved when he'd called to let her know he and Dusty were on their way up, and she'd said that if she wasn't there when they arrived that one of the grad students would fill them in. He'd thought she meant at the supermarket or something, but now he realized she'd probably been planning to go to Willow Creek but hadn't wanted to say so on the phone. He hadn't told her what had transpired on the road, since she had enough to worry about without him adding how they had been accosted by persons unknown at that turnout on the 101.

Once at the barn, he struggled to open the large double doors. Dusty had to help him by holding one while Lester pulled the other. When Danny and Oliver saw Lester step into the dimly lit barn, the men had to cover their ears from the din. Oliver pounded the bars with his fists, and Danny raced back and forth, slapping his feet on the concrete floor, hooting, and screaming. Lester paused to let his eyes adjust. Streams of sunlight filtered through the cracks between the plank siding and holes in the corrugated-tin roof. Lester motioned to Dusty to remain outside and hold the door open to give more light.

When Lester's eyes adjusted, he saw several handlers surrounding the steel-barred cage striking the bars with canes. A young man loaded a dart gun. His hands shook so much that he could hardly fill the syringe with ketamine. Oliver and Danny screamed, showing all their teeth. Their coarse black hair bristled, making them appear larger. Danny lunged at the bars, his hands and feet pushing through them, trying to grab the handlers, but his powerful hands grasped nothing but air. One of the braver handlers tried to hit Oliver's outstretched arm. In a blur, Oliver grabbed the oak cane and broke it in two like a toothpick.

Lester neared the cage and whispered to himself, "They're displaying fear grimaces and piloerecting . . . They're afraid." In a commanding voice, he yelled, "Stop this! What do you think you're doing?"

The handlers looked from one to the other before one answered, "Mrs. Turner received a note from Dr. Turner telling us to get them ready to move them out of here." He paused before continuing, "Something about a surprise inspection."

"He sure didn't mean for you idiots to try to move them yourselves! I want all of you to clear out!" Lester yelled.

The handlers looked from one to another, hesitating. A booming voice startled them when it rose up from behind them and commanded them over the screams, "You heard the man! Everyone needs to leave the barn, now!"

The handlers left the barn, heads down, careful not to look at Lester. One handed Dusty the dart gun.

"What the hell do I do with this?" Dusty asked.

"Lay it out of sight," Lester said as he walked up to the cage door.

"You want me in or out?" Dusty asked as he looked longingly at the only way out of the barn.

"Close the door. I can use some help manning the transfer box," Lester said as he motioned Dusty toward the box.

Danny and Oliver raced to the door and signed, "Out, out." But they both backed away from the door when Lester neared.

Dusty sighed and wiped his forehead with the back of his jacket sleeve before he climbed on top of the transfer cage. He realized that the whole crew of handlers was watching them through the cracks of the barn. He knew exactly what Lester had planned. He'd seen the practice hundreds of times at animal compounds and zoos around the world, but he wasn't excited to help Lester move these freaks of nature from their large steel cage to the smaller transfer box. He smirked when he read the large stenciled warning in red: WATC—Danger Wild Animals. *Where's Dr. Raven when we need him?*

Dusty was an elephant trainer and hated working with primates and big cats, which is what this procedure was designed for. The smaller movable box was chained to the bars of the larger cage, and its guillotine door would be slid down to close the animals inside once they'd been coaxed into the box. The procedure had caused the death of countless trainers, many that Dusty had known. It only took one thing to go wrong to get you killed. If the box wasn't chained tight enough, the animal could reach you through the gap and strain you thorough the bars of the cage. Or if something failed or broke, you'd have a loose, raging animal climbing up the box to chase you. However, Lester was the best in the business, and Dusty'd trust his life to his skill.

Lester reached for the lock, looking back at Dusty. "Where the hell are the keys?"

Dusty realized he still held the keys a handler had given him on his way out. He tossed them in the direction of his friend, but they landed short, near Lester's feet. Lester dove his hand deep into the thick hay, searching for them while cussing under his breath and keeping an eye on Danny and Oliver. Finally, he found them.

"Hell, we're getting nowhere with this craziness." Lester took a deep breath, looked back at Dusty, and with a smile, put the key to the lock and opened the cage.

Dusty looked back toward the barn door—the only way out—and said, "Shit." But thinking better of it, he climbed down from the top of the transfer cage and held the door behind Lester, ready to latch and close it. Danny and Oliver stood up without a sound, their hair puffed up as they walked toward Lester.

Dusty was struck by how small Lester appeared standing next to these giants. They towered a shoulder above Lester's six-foot frame. Dusty tried to remember where he'd laid the dart gun, but before he could do anything, both creatures apprehensively moved in and greeted Lester.

Lester looked at Danny, pointed to the ground and commanded, "Sit!"

To Dusty's amazement, Danny settled into the deep hay, his arms folded and his feet straight out. Oliver raced toward Lester, his lips curled back showing all his teeth, including two larger canines.

Lester turned, opened his arms, and said, "Give me a big hug, old friend."

Oliver engulfed Lester with his muscular arms. Oliver's mouth covered the whole side of Lester's face and neck, his long canines dimpling his cheek and throat as he panted.

Lester laughed and thumped Oliver on his back with a closed fist. "All right, good boy!"

Oliver stepped back, pointed to the door, and signed, "Out, out."

Lester looked at Oliver for a moment and shook his head as he kicked clumps of hay, before he signed, "No. In, in."

Oliver whimpered but slowly made his way into the transfer box. Lester pointed to Danny and without a word signed, "Follow."

Danny rose, facing Lester, his lips tightly covering his teeth. He moved slowly and hesitated when Lester stepped toward him. Confused, Danny looked from Lester to Oliver. He whimpered and hooted kend looked at the door to the cage and signed, "Out!"

Lester shook his head. "No, old friend. Not now. We're

going on a trip. A long trip."

Danny sat down in the deep hay.

Lester grinned, shaking his head. "No, old friend. You're going in." He stepped toward Danny, pointing toward the cage.

Danny whimpered and hesitated, but he went in, and Dusty slid the guillotine door down, securing both creatures safely into the transfer cage. Applause broke out from all around the outside of the barn as the handlers pounded the sides of the wooden barn. Dusty smiled to himself, realizing he'd just witnessed the making of a legend. *This'll be a story told for generations. These kids just witnessed the best chimp trainer in the world at his best.*

Lester nodded toward Dusty and said, "Where's Girlie?"

"Shit!" Dusty replied, racing out the barn door.

Lester followed, mumbling to himself, hands in his pockets.

Outside, he squinted against the bright sunlight as Dusty closed the barn door behind them. As Lester's eyes adjusted, he noticed several handlers gathering around. Many reached out to touch Lester, almost as though they wanted to feel the magic they'd witnessed. Lester ignored them and walked back toward the trailer into which they'd load the transfer cage.

Dusty raced over and fired up the Willys, then backed it toward the trailer to hook it up to the old, rusting rig. Though they'd just arrived, Lester knew as well as Dusty that there was no reason to stick around, especially with Mary not there.

The grad student who had greeted them at the house strode up to Lester and said, "Thanks for that. There's a message from Mary I have to give you." He paused.

Lester frowned. "Well, what is it?"

He shrugged. "It's a bit cryptic, but she said you'd know what it meant. She phoned just after she'd left and said she'd received a message from Dr. Turner asking you to send the package to curiosity killed the cat."

Lester chuckled. It was Ken's curiosity that got them into his mess in the first place. "Message received." He wandered over to the Willys Wagon and was surprised to see Girlie sitting in the back seat. She hooted and bounced so hard when she saw him that she rocked the entire vehicle. Lester smiled. "Easy girl."

Girlie hooted again, forming her lips like a trumpet, then sat back down and folded her arms.

Lester ignored the racket as, once Dusty had the unmarked horse trailer hooked up, the handlers loaded the transfer cage containing Danny and Oliver into it. Lester wondered if the old rig could pull such a big trailer. There was only one way to know and that was to do it.

Lester looked over at Dusty and said, "Let's see if this piece of junk is up to towing."

Dusty flipped him off with the one-finger salute and growled, "What are you calling a piece of shit?" He walked around the Willys and gently stroked the fender and hood before getting in.

Lester laughed and took a moment to take in the assembled rig—an old, rusting Willys hooked to a brand-new aluminum trailer. The trailer was absent of all markings except *Sooner* in red cursive. He looked over at Dusty and said, "Well, I guess we're traveling in style. Shit, a Sooner is the Airstream of horse trailers. So I'll ask you again, will this rusting heap make it to Willow Creek?"

Without a word, Dusty settled in his rig, coughed it into life, and revved it in stuttering roars. He cranked down the window and yelled, "If we're going, let's get going!" The trailer rocked, its springs squeaking, and Danny and Oliver hooted and bounced. Girlie looked over her shoulder back at the trailer and panted, then she smiled and pointed in the direction of the 395.

Dusty revved the engine and engaged the gears with a jarring grind. The rear wheels spun to life, throwing up bits of gravel that rattled into the wheel wells. Lester jumped in at the last minute, and Girlie leaned in between both trainers from the back seat. She gently put her arms around each of them and pointed again toward Highway 395. Both trainers laughed and settled in for a long ride. They had a lot to do and a long way to go, and they didn't know where or how this adventure would end, but they knew one thing for sure: they would not abandon Oliver or Danny. They would see this through to the end.

The trailer squeaked and groaned as they made their way out along the ranch's dirt drive, then they turned left onto Holcomb Avenue, which wound through pastureland and out to the highway. Girlie lay down in the back and pulled a blanket over herself, and Danny and Oliver seemed to quieten down as they hit the rhythm of the traffic on 395. They headed north through downtown Reno and took a turn onto the two-lane highway that hugged the Feather River and wound north through Plumas National Forest. Their unmarked rig would blend in here in horse country—comforting to know—as they made their way to Willow Creek and the wilderness along the Trinity River.

Chapter Thirty-One

Lester swung open the double doors of the converted horse trailer. Danny and Oliver leaned against the steel bars and stuck their arms out, making begging gestures. *Very chimplike*, Lester thought.

Oliver gazed out across the clearing where they'd camped, looking toward the forest line, and signed, "Out, out."

Lester shook his head. "Not yet, old friend."

Oliver whimpered, and Danny stomped his feet on the metal floor, making loud booms that filled the meadow. They both bellowed hoots and pounded their fists against the steel bars.

Dusty took in the surroundings. "I'm glad we pulled over here. Those damn things are making way too much noise."

Lester nodded. "Hopefully we're okay here. Ever since we had those thugs show up, I've felt we're being followed."

Dusty frowned. "So what the hell are we doing out here?"

Lester paused from feeding and watering. "Dusty, I knew both these chimps when they were still youngsters. I'm going to decide what should happen to them."

"I know that look. Just tell me what we're going to do."

"I want to find Ken and find a place to set them free." Lester scanned their surroundings, his hand shading his eyes against the morning sun.

"Why this area?" Dusty shifted his weight from one foot to the other.

Lester pointed at a rusting sign on the edge of the turnout that welcomed them to the Hupa Reservation. "This is Indian country, and people don't visit it very often." He pointed at Oliver and Danny. "I think these two could do pretty well out in this territory. Hell, they say Bigfoot lives in this forest."

Dusty raised his hands. "Yeah, right. Bigfoot!"

Lester ignored Dusty as he finished stacking the bags of monkey chow out of the way of the door. He looked up from his work and said, "You best get in the wagon. I need to open the door to feed and water them."

Dusty raced to the old Willys and slammed the door behind him. He rolled up the windows as Lester fumbled around with his ring of keys.

Dusty searched the glove box and yelled, "Where's the guns we took off those guys that tried to roll us?"

"Never mind, it'd just piss them off. Just lay low until I get them settled."

Lester returned to the cage door at the back of the horse trailer. Danny and Oliver jumped up and down when he reached for the padlock, hooting in high-pitched screams of excitement. Oliver kept signing "Out" over and over, while Danny swaggered side to side, flapping his feet and leaning on his knuckles. Lester stopped and stared at them. They both froze, whimpering like young chimps.

"That's better," Lester said. "Let's see some manners. Feet!" They sat and both crossed their arms around their chests and extended their legs straight out. It was a command Lester had used his whole career to make sure he had control of the apes he was handling.

He opened the door and stepped in carrying a jug of water. Oliver raced over and engulfed him with a big hug. Danny stood back, tilting his head. Lester signed, "Good boys?"

Both signed back almost in unison, "Good." Each made a smacking noise as they kissed the palms of their hands while making the sign.

Suddenly, Dusty honked the horn and yelled, "We've got company!"

Lester looked over his shoulder. A black SUV skidded to a stop behind them and several men dressed in fatigues piled out, armed with rifles. Before he, Dusty, or the men could do anything, Danny shoved Lester aside, raced toward the SUV, and attacked in a blur. Screams rose up in the clearing but faded as quickly as they'd begun. By the time Danny backed off and the dust settled, the men lay motionless like broken dolls. The suburban was empty, its engine still running.

Lester and Dusty stood looking at the carnage in disbelief.

"How did this happen so quickly?" Dusty asked in a shocked voice.

"It happened," Lester said as he motioned Oliver to go back into the trailer.

Oliver hesitated, his lips tight against his teeth as he looked across the clearing toward the mountains that rose up in what looked like the heart of the Hupa Reservation. He held Lester's eyes for several heartbeats, shook his head and signed, "No." He pointed up toward the mountains. A mist rose from the summit. All was quiet in the meadow that skirted the dense forest of ferns and pines.

Oliver turned and struck out across the grassy meadow toward the shadows of the tree line, throwing one last look back over his shoulder.

Lester and Dusty stood speechless.

Danny looked from Lester to Oliver with a quizzical expression as if unsure of what to do next.

Lester sighed, then shrugged and signed, "All right. Go now."

Danny hesitated, then followed but stopped about halfway between the forest and Lester. He kneeled, looking back and forth and whimpering.

Oliver stopped, turned around, walked upright back across the clearing, and put his giant hand on Danny's shoulder. He tapped him gently and signed, "Go now. Safe over there."

Danny glanced one last time at Lester before he followed Oliver across the meadow. They disappeared into the shadows of the woods, their passing as ephemeral as a gust of wind.

Dusty closed the cage doors with a clang and latched the double doors of the trailer. "Well, that's that."

Still staring in the direction of the forest, Lester said, "I wonder." He wiped off tears with the back of his calloused hand.

Dusty fired up the old Willys. "Come on, we need to get the hell out of here and warn Ken and the others."

Lester gazed out at the mountains that rose up from the thickets of trees and whispered, "I think this was meant to be. There's more at work here than chance. We were drawn here." He climbed into the Willys and looked in the back seat to find Girlie rocking as she made slight trumpet hoots.

She caught Lester's eyes and signed, "Go now. Hurry."

Lester nodded. "Okay, Dusty, if we're going, let's get going before someone shows up."

Dusty nodded, but then pointed at the suburban. "Should we check on things?"

"Hell no. Let's get going."

Without another word, Dusty floored it, racing out in a cloud of dust.

Chapter Thirty-Two

"Well, that didn't go particularly well, did it?" Consuelo said as they left the sheriff's office. "Spies? Honestly."

"He caught me off guard," Mary said. "I wasn't prepared for him to ask *us* questions."

"Well, now we know he hasn't seen them, or this ranger fellow, or any of Vandusen's men, presumably," Chris said as they walked back toward the motel.

"I'm not sure he would've told us if he had," Mary said. "We need to do our own investigating." When they walked up the path to the motel, she took ahold of Consuelo's arm and whispered, "Go to the front office and see what you can find out, especially who our guys may have spoken to, or where they may have disappeared to."

Consuelo nodded and left without a word.

Back in her room, Mary flopped onto one of the beds with a sigh and began counting the water stains on the ceiling. She was just about to comment when there was a knock at the door. She opened it to find Consuelo standing there with a tall bearded man. Mary gestured them to come inside and closed the door behind them, wondering if all the people in this little community looked like Jeremiah Johnson.

The man cast furtive glances around the room, being careful not to make eye contact with anyone. Mary wondered why he was so nervous but decided to act as though she didn't notice. "Who do we have here?" she said to Consuelo.

Consuelo smiled. "This is Willy, the motel manager. He has something to share with us."

Willy looked from Chris to Mary, hesitating to speak. Mary nodded toward him and smiled. Willy cleared his throat and stuttered a few words.

"I'm sorry, Willy. I didn't get that," Mary said in her calmest tone. She motioned him to take a seat, and Consuelo brought him a bottle of water. Mary noticed his hands shook as he reached for it. She smiled and said, "Let's try this again. What can you tell us about our friends?"

Willy looked down at the worn rug, took a deep breath, and said, "They were here for several days and took up with a couple of locals."

"Locals?" Mary asked.

"Yes, a Hupa named Jimmy Two-Feathers, and Randy, the owner of our local Bigfoot bookstore. Randy's our local expert on Bigfoot and such."

"A what? Hupa, did you say?" Mary asked.

Willy's eyes locked onto Chris. Apparently, he felt more comfortable ignoring Mary and Consuelo. "The Hupa are the local Indian tribe around here," he said. "They've believed in Bigfoot clear back to ancient times. And Jimmy is a real true believer. He claims to have seen one, if you can believe that."

"You say my husband 'took up with' this Jimmy Two-Feathers?" She cursed to herself when she saw Willy look up for an instant when she said *husband*. The less any of these people in town knew about them, the better. "So where are they now?"

Willy nodded to Mary and replied, "I heard he led

your . . . husband and his company into the wilderness to look for Bigfoot."

Mary noticed he made a slight pause when he referred to Ken. She moved on, changing the subject. "What about this other person, the bookstore owner?"

"Oh, Randy, you mean? He's got a little bookstore up the main highway with a huge section on Bigfoot. He's very active with the kooks, ah, people interested in Bigfoot."

"I take it you don't go in for all this stuff about Bigfoot?" Mary said, smiling.

"I just never seen one . . . They're good for business, though."

"Right, where's this bookstore at?"

***

Mary thought the bookstore looked more like an abandoned thrift shop than an actual place of business. The smell when they entered was that of dusty books, and they had to pause to let their eyes adjust in the dim light. At first they didn't notice the man sitting behind the counter piled with books. He looked up with interest but waited for someone to speak.

"Good afternoon," Mary said.

"How can I help you?" the man said. His face opened with his question and made his buggy eyes even rounder.

His comical expression amused Mary and she worked hard not to laugh outright. "I'm . . . I'm sorry. I seemed to have lost my train of thought. Ah, yes. We've found ourselves separated from our friends and are trying to find someone who can help us reunite."

"Are you referring to the party that left with Jimmy Two-Feathers?"

"Yes!" everyone answered in unison.

He surveyed the group, stood up, sliding a stool on casters aside, and nodded toward a forest service map on the wall. "They're making their way to Bluff Creek, is my guess."

Mary frowned. "To where?"

"It's where the Patterson-Gimli footage of Bigfoot was captured," Tamara explained.

The shopkeeper broke into a smile. "Well, someone knows our local history. That red pin with the worn spot surrounding it is where the site is located."

Chris walked over to take a closer look and the rest followed, including Randy. They stood in silence for several minutes as each tried to trace a route with their fingers.

Finally, Randy broke the silence. "There's a logging road that splits off just before the stream crossing. If you follow that a couple of miles, you'll find that new primate compound."

The group looked knowingly at each other.

Randy grinned, noticing their glances, and traced his finger over the route on the worn map.

"I wonder what they're doing out there," Mary said as they all looked at the green that marked the wilderness surrounding the red pin.

Randy chuckled. "Looking for Bigfoot, of course."

Mary shot a glance at Chris. "Perhaps they've found them."

"Either way, I expect they're on their way back by now," Randy said.

As they walked out of the store, Mary said to Sandy, "We need to try that ranger's number again."

***

Kelly picked up the phone on the second ring and wrapped a towel around himself. Steam had filled the closed-in sitting area of the Airstream. He'd taken a long shower to wash the mud and grime from his recon mission. "This is Kelly," he answered in a strained voice, then relaxed when he heard Sandy's voice on the other end.

"So you're back," Sandy said.

"Yeah," Kelly replied. "I had a look around that new primate center the government is building out at the old logging camp." Images of his adventure flashed as he waited for that to sink in with Lt. Sandy. After several heartbeats he broke the silence. "Are you still there?"

"We're over at the motel."

Kelly dropped the towel and grabbed his trousers off the floor. "I'm on my way."

***

The agent put his earphones down and asked, "Shall we pick them up? Sounds like the ranger is headed to that dumpy little motel in town. Besides Turner's wife, I'm not sure who else might be there."

Vandusen shook his head. "Not yet." He looked around the radio room the general had funded—a great conversion of the old toolshed. This listening post was better than one he'd used at Fort Devens with the Army Security Agency during Nam. Bauer had converted this run-down old logging camp into a state-of-the-art base camp. Life was good, if you could stay on the good side of the general.

When he realized the agent was still waiting for him to elaborate, he sneered and said, "Let's wait and make sure we get all our little peace doves into one nest." He smiled, picturing just how he'd welcome Turner and company.

The agent gave a thumbs-up, guessing what his boss was

thinking, then returned to monitoring the radio and telephone traffic coming in and out of the little town of Willow Creek. Out here in the sticks, that task wasn't very hard.

Vandusen was worried, though. He knew that the fucking plane crash would bring on some heat, but he hadn't figure on his old friend Dr. Turner being part of the bargain. This operation was getting complicated, and the general didn't like complications. Vandusen was going to have to fix this before the general got wind of it. He swore under his breath and stepped outside. Bauer was waiting by the door. "Put a tail on those assholes in Willow Creek, but don't pick them up yet. They're all persons of interest."

Bauer nodded. "Are we gonna pick up everyone?"

"Yes, but not before we grab that sheriff and ranger along with Mrs. Turner and friends." Vandusen lit a Lucky Strike and spat some pieces of tobacco out before he continued, "We'll make it clean, and not leave any loose ends. Understood?"

Bauer snapped to attention. "Yes, sir!"

Vandusen nodded toward the door. "Go inside and get what intelligence we have on them." He waited for Bauer to close the door behind him before he headed over to their new observation room.

Chapter Thirty-Three

"Don't worry, I'll find them," Kelly reassured Mary. "I know the routes Jimmy takes. They shouldn't be far away now, and I can take a detour on the way back so they can see what's happening at that old logging camp."

"No," Mary said, eyes wide with fear. "I don't want him anywhere near there."

"I agree," Consuelo said. "If Vandusen sees him, he'll kill him without a thought. And the others." She bit her lip.

Tamara got up and paced the room.

Chris shook his head. "You won't be able to stop them. Once Kelly here has told them what he told us, Ken and Fred will want to see it. They'll be able to identify the creatures from their cries."

Mary groaned. "But you could try to dissuade them, couldn't you?" She looked at Kelly.

He nodded. "I'll let them know that you would prefer it if they all came straight back here."

Sandy stood. "So when do we leave?"

Kelly shook his head. "Not *we*, *me*. You'll just slow me down."

Sandy sighed, cast a look at himself, then at Kelly's trim, athletic figure and sat back down.

"What about me?" Chris said. "I'd like to see this place, and I'm fit. I could keep up."

"Are you used to this country?" Kelly asked. "Thick forest? Not to mention staying out of sight of those you'd rather not see you. Like these creatures you think escaped from that plane."

Chris grimaced.

"I thought as much, so no. Thanks for the offer, but I work better alone, and the best thing is to get to your friends as soon as possible and give them the intel you gave me." He stood to leave. "But first, I need to check in with the sheriff. Lt. Sandy, would you like to do the same?"

Sandy nodded and stood again. "We can decide how much to tell him on the way."

"Just don't mention the creatures," Mary said.

"Don't worry, ma'am," Kelly said. "I didn't intend to."

"Or research spies," Consuelo added.

"What?"

"Never mind," Chris said. "Just go. Find them and keep them safe."

Chapter Thirty-Four

Kelly couldn't believe how much the old logging camp had changed since he'd sneaked into it. It was obvious by the new towers and finished fence line that security had been increased. It wouldn't be possible to make another clandestine visit. The place was crawling with military. A tap on his shoulder startled him. He relaxed when he realized that Ken and his crew had finally caught up. One of their crew had been lagging behind all day and had slowed their progress.

"Sorry, but one of our team, Hunt, is really having trouble keeping up," Ken whispered.

"Well, we're here now, but we can't camp anywhere near this facility. As you can see, they're sending patrols out all around this area. Take a look." Kelly pointed down toward a small group of soldiers exiting the front gate. Barking echoed up the hill to where they crouched. "It's time to haul ass! Those are K-9 patrol dogs. Maybe we can get closer if we wait until it's dark," Kelly said as he led the group back into the shadows of the forest.

***

Low-flying clouds settled around them, making the evening

warmer than the previous few nights in the forest. Even the drips from the sagging branches felt lukewarm. Ken was relieved to see Hunt regaining some of his energy. It had been slow going, a crawl really, with Hunt struggling to keep up with them, and his coughing fits sent the whole group into a panic. It felt as if something in the forest listened to them and was watching their every move.

Ken nudged Kelly and whispered, "Is it safe to work our way down for a closer look now?"

Kelly crawled over the boulder they'd hunkered behind, and after few moments, nodded.

"Okay, let's do it," Ken said.

The group picked their way, single file, along the faint tracings of what looked like a deer path toward the bright lights of the primate facility. Though they remained high above the facility and still a safe distance from it, they had to cover their eyes against the glare. Ghost-like figures marched along the fence line, and a search light arced from the watchtowers. They ducked when the beam crossed near them.

"I've never seen a primate center like this," Mark whispered.

"It's guarded like a goddamn prison," Fred said.

Kelly pointed at the towers. "Look, some of the guards are facing in. This place is designed to keep people in, as well as out."

Ken winced. "You're sure Dr. Melon and his family are in there?"

"As I told you, I actually talked to your Dr. Melon, but I never met his family. I just overheard some of the workers talking about them."

Fred strained over Ken's shoulder and said, "We'll never get in there."

"We may not have to." Bobby pointed at a hillside across from them.

Danny and Oliver stepped out of the darkness near the back of the compound.

Ken stood up to shout a warning, but Hunt pulled him back. "There's nothing we can do from here. Just watch!"

"What the hell are they doing?" Fred said. "And how did they get here?"

"I thought Dusty and Lester had them!" Ken said.

Kelly looked at him with a puzzled frown.

"Never mind that," Bobby whispered. "Look what's behind them!"

A large group of tall, hairy creatures came out of the darkness to join Oliver and Danny.

Kelly shook his head. "I never thought I'd see one, let alone a whole tribe of them."

"Those are not the creatures we found in Africa," Ken observed.

"No," Fred said, eyes wide. "It must be a tribe of bigfoots."

Mark shook his head in amazement. "*And* they've surrounded the place. Look at the forest line all around."

They scanned the forest line. The bigfoots stood, unmoving like sentinels, spaced at regular intervals. Some bent and picked up large rocks. Others held a rock in their hands already.

"Rocks?" Bobby whispered. "What the hell?"

Ken pointed back to Danny and Oliver. A group of creatures emerged silently from the forest behind them. "Look over there," Ken said. "Those are the creatures we've been tracking."

"My god! Bigfoots and the creatures together out here in the forest," Bobby said.

"*And* Danny and Oliver," Hunt said.

Oliver gestured for the group to spread out.

One of the soldiers shouted, and shots rang out.

At the same time, the bigfoots threw their rocks onto the minefield Kelly had discovered. Multiple explosions echoed across the canyon and from all around the compound. The bigfoots picked up more rocks and kept hurling them until the explosions stopped, then the creatures, led by Oliver and Danny, raced toward the fence under the cover of the flying dirt and dust clouds. The bigfoots strode down after them.

Several of the creatures ripped through the fence like it was tennis netting and attacked the soldiers while they were disoriented from the explosions. Screams of the men rose above the gunshots. A bigfoot ripped the double gates off their hinges and stomped on them, sending bellowing hoots into the night. Another pulled at a tower footing until it came tumbling down.

Soon the whole compound was filled with bigfoots and the creatures.

"Look at the bigfoots," Fred said.

Mark nodded. "I noticed that too. They're not attacking the people. Just destroying the buildings."

"The creatures are doing all the slaughtering," Bobby said.

Hunt threw up in somewhere behind them.

Oliver and Danny had led the creatures in an attack so savage that it unnerved even those who'd seen the destruction in Africa. The screams took on a higher pitch.

Ken whispered, "It's just like Africa." He searched his colleagues' faces, still lit by the glow of the lights, before continuing, "My god, what have we done?"

"Nothing," Fred replied. "Vandusen brought these creatures here and managed to let them loose."

"But Danny and Oliver leading them?" Ken shook his head. "I can't watch this." He turned his back to the horrors below.

"Dr. Melon is somewhere down there," Hunt whispered.

"Good," Fred said as he strapped his backpack closed.

Kelly pulled himself out of his state of shock and pointed at the house on the hill. "That's where Melon lives—and his family."

Ken turned back. "We can't leave them to these creatures." He took a breath, steeled himself for action, and headed down the game trail that led toward the facility.

"Christ!" Fred said and struck out after Ken.

The rest gathered their equipment and followed.

Kelly raced after Ken, grabbed his arm, handed him his rifle, and said, "I'm going to hump it back to my truck and radio for backup." Before Ken could respond, the ranger disappeared into the darkness.

Ken shook his head, cocked the lever on the 30-30, and continued down the game trail. The rest followed him toward the chaos below. Ken feared that by the time they got there, it would be too late.

Chapter Thirty-Five

"Roger that!" The sheriff paused for a moment, staring into space as he gathered his thoughts.

A knock sounded on his door. He jumped, then took a deep breath before he opened his door and motioned his secretary inside. By the look on her face, he'd have to act cool and calm despite how he felt. He managed a smile and worked to keep his manner calm before he spoke. "We need to all stay cool and professional. Kelly is going to be fine. I can't think of anyone I'd rather have out there right now. I need you to call in anyone off-duty and get them in here, ASAP. Keep what we heard on the radio to ourselves. I'll talk to the crew all together when we get them assembled. Understand?"

"Yes, sir," the secretary responded in a quivering voice before turning to leave the room.

"Wait!" the sheriff yelled. "Get me the number for the Bigfoot Motel." He held his hand up, stopping the secretary from speaking, and continued, "I think we better get our visitors in the loop."

She nodded and raced down the hallway toward her desk in the reception area. The sheriff sighed and unlocked the weapons cabinet.

***

Mary slammed the phone down so hard it rang.

Consuelo got up from the bed where she'd been sitting and asked, "What's wrong?" She scooted next to Mary and put her arm over Mary's shoulder.

Mary brushed a strand of her red hair back from her face and paused, looking at everyone in the room. Her voice broke at first when she tried to speak, but she finally brought it and herself under control and said in the most level tone she could manage, "There's been an incident at that DOD facility. According to the sheriff, Ken and the rest of our group were involved." Mary let that set in before she continued, "He doesn't know what has happened or if they're safe or not."

Everyone sat in silence. Though they'd been dreading a call like this, they still needed time to process it. Mary broke the silence and said, "We need to get moving. The sheriff wants to see us."

"I hope not to identify the bodies!" Consuelo said, her eyes moistening.

Sandy raised his chin and whispered, "Let's not jump to any conclusions. I think if they could survive Africa, we sure as hell can get through this."

Chris stood and picked up his backpack. "He's right. Let's go find Willow Creek's finest and do what we can."

The group sprang into action, gathering their belongings and making ready for the deputy the sheriff had said would pick them up. A knock on the door startled them.

"That must be the deputy already," Tamara said.

To their surprise, she opened the door to Dusty and Lester.

"What in the hell are you doing here?" Chris said. "You're supposed to be with Oliver and Danny!"

Lester and Dusty hesitated before Lester took the lead and said, "Well, we're kinda done with that job."

Before anyone could speak, they were prodded into action by a horn honking in the parking lot next to the rusty Bigfoot cage, the main tourist attraction at the motel.

Chapter Thirty-Six

Ken and company stood under the one remaining light of the facility, looking at the destruction in horror. The creatures had torn the main gates off their hinges, left gaping holes in the wire of the perimeter fence, and smashed all the doors and windows. The towers lay in rubble. Smoke rose from the shattered search lights, and every building had walls that had been kicked in or torn down, making them unusable.

"Well," Mark said, "seems the bigfoots sent a clear message that they don't want this facility here."

"Is that what this is?" Fred asked.

"It's as if they left this one light so we could see what they did," Bobby said grimly.

"So far as I could see, the bigfoots only destroyed the buildings and infrastructure," Mark pointed out. "It was the creatures that did all this." He gestured at the dismembered corpses scattered around.

"Territorial behavior?" Fred asked.

Ken shook his head. "For the bigfoots, perhaps, but listen. What do you hear?"

"Nothing," several of them said at the same time.

"Exactly," Ken said. "But before all this started, we heard

creatures down here. It sounds to me like they've gone."

"Escaped," Hunt whispered.

"Or rescued," Ken said.

The track down from their vantage point had passed through a gully, which meant their view of the facility had been obscured for most of the way. They'd heard cries, screams, gunshots, and glass and wood shattering until it had finally fallen silent. Given what they'd seen and heard, the bodies that lay scattered around didn't surprise anyone. What did surprise Ken was that the only corpses were human. Had the creatures carried off their dead? Surely they didn't all escape the hail of bullets.

Bobby kneeled to examine the body of a soldier who lay in a twisted heap. Looking up, he wiped his face with his sleeve and said, "This reminds me of Africa." He searched through the corpse's pockets. "There's no identification on him."

The rest began searching the other dead but found nothing that would connect any of them to any organization.

Ken looked up at the house on the hill where Kelly had said Dr. Melon and his family lived. "That doesn't look too damaged. I'm going to see if Melon survived." He headed off, and the others interrupted their search and followed him.

They stopped at the shattered gate of the small picket fence surrounding the front flower garden, now trampled into mud. Ken sighed. "Maybe not so undamaged."

"And yet the windows are intact," Fred pointed out.

Ken frowned, puzzled. "Maybe they didn't see the inhabitants as a threat."

"Or maybe there's no one here," Bobby said.

They walked up to the door, but found it locked.

"Dr. Melon!" Ken yelled. "Are you in there? It's Dr. Turner. It's all over. You're safe now. Open the door."

No answer.

"Dr. Melon? . . . Hello?"

They waited, but nothing stirred, and no sound broke the silence.

"See if you can find an open window," Fred said, but though they walked all around the residence, no one could find an open window either.

Ken scratched his head. "What now?"

"Maybe they aren't here," Hunt said.

Kelly's jeep pulled into the camp. He jumped out and jogged over to them. "What's up?"

"Locked," Ken said.

Without a word, Kelly kicked open the door.

"That works," Bobby muttered.

It took a moment for their eyes to adjust to the dark house, then they searched the rooms, but they found no one. Ken turned to leave, but Kelly grabbed his arm and said, "If I remember correctly, there's a basement," The ranger nodded toward a closet door off the kitchen. "I used to come here when I was a kid. My dad worked as a truck driver before the camp closed down."

Ken opened the door and looked down into the darkness. He would have fallen down the steep stairs had Kelly not pulled him back. "Hello, is anyone down there?" he shouted, his voice echoing off the concrete walls below.

The smell of damp, stale air assaulted him as he made his way down the stairs with Kelly behind him. At the bottom he fumbled around in the darkness until he found the chain of an overhanging lightbulb and pulled on it. Pale light flooded the cellar. The lightbulb swung on a frayed wire above them, casting swirling shadows against shelves of dusty mason jars.

Ken handed Kelly his rifle and motioned him to follow. "Is anyone down here? Dr. Melon, it's Dr. Ken Turner."

They heard someone, or something, stir under a workbench.

Kelly pushed Ken to one side and leveled his rifle in the direction of the noise.

"Hold on!" Ken kneeled and pulled aside a pile of chairs.

The bulb cast just enough light to illuminate Dr. Melon, his wife, and his daughter huddled together. Dr. Melon tried to speak but could only move his quivering lips. The young girl leaned away from them, crying.

"You're safe now. You can come with us," Ken said as he reached for Dr. Melon's trembling hands.

Kelly cleared the rest of the debris so they could get out.

***

The sheriff hadn't said a word since Mary had convinced him to take her and her group with him. He hadn't planned on taking them anywhere, saying they'd only get in the way if they came along. Apparently, he'd only wanted to question them to see if they could shed any light on the situation, as he called it. But he hadn't told them much, just that Ranger Kelly had called and said that Ken and his group were with him at the DOD facility and there'd been a violent incident perpetrated by—he'd paused there as if having difficulty getting the words out—a group of animals that looked a lot like Bigfoot.

When she hurriedly told him about their theories as to the cause of the massacre and explained that they had prior experience and expertise in dealing with the creatures that may or may not be related to Bigfoot, he relented, but she had a sense it was more to keep an eye on them than because he believed anything she'd said. She'd caught him glancing in the rearview mirror at them as he negotiated the ruts in the narrow dirt road that snaked its way through the forest. After all this clandestine maneuvering, they were finally on their way to the secret DOD facility. She didn't like the circumstances leading them there, though, and she had no idea what they'd find when they got there. She took several deep breaths to calm herself.

Consuelo reached over and squeezed her shoulder and attempted to reassure her with a wilted smile.

Mary laid her head against the window and shut her eyes. She didn't like how dark and closed-in the forest was, preferring streetlights and sidewalks. She tried to think of other things besides what might've happened to Ken.

After what seemed like hours of bumping and jiggling over endless hills and curves, the road flattened out and they slowed down. She shaded her eyes against the glare of the morning sun and gasped at the sight before them. The camp lay in ruins.

"My god, what happened here?" Mary asked.

The sheriff stood behind the open door of his Wagoneer and motioned to the group to stay inside. He pulled his revolver out and slowly walked into the facility, picking his way around the tangled gates that lay with the rest of the debris on the ground.

Sandy got out without a word and joined the sheriff, and they made their way to a group standing on the porch of a residence that seemed out of place with its picket fence and flower garden. The glare of the early morning sun made it hard to make out any other details.

A knock on the window startled Lester and Dusty. The deputy accompanying them peered inside and gestured at them to follow them. They got out of the Wagoneer and headed up to the house with the picket fence.

***

Dr. Melon sat on the steps in front of the house, staring into space. His head and hands shook as he tried to sip the cup of coffee Hunt had made for him. They could hear rattling dishes in the kitchen through the window off the porch where everyone had gathered around Melon, his wife, and daughter.

The sheriff made a clicking noise with his tongue. It was a nervous habit he had that had always annoyed Kelly. Now it was annoying the whole group. Kelly threw his hands up and said, "They're all in shock. We're not going to get anything out of them right now."

The sheriff wrinkled his forehead. "This is a crime scene, and they're the only people left alive in it. Their testimony is vital to understanding what happened here."

Ken made his way up the steps after untangling himself from Mary. When he'd seen her coming, he'd run across the grounds and they'd embraced, separating themselves from the others. Mark and Consuelo had done the same, and everyone, including the sheriff and his deputies, had kept their distance. Now Ken kneeled on the steps, touched Melon's arm, and whispered, "Dr. Melon, what's been going on here?"

Melon looked up at the faces that stared down at him as though noticing everyone for the first time. "We've been prisoners here," he replied in an unsteady voice. "We couldn't come or go, and all our communications had to go through them. We've not been allowed visitors or contact with the outside world for over—"

A frail voice interrupted, "Six months." Melon's wife hugged her daughter and yelled, "They were going to let those monsters have their way with us!"

"What monsters are you talking about?" the sheriff asked.

Kelly held his hand up to stop the sheriff from continuing and said, "You're safe now. They're gone."

Melon's daughter began to weep. Melon and his wife leaned their heads on her shoulder.

Mary pushed through, waving at everyone to step back. "Give these poor people some room. Can't you see they need some time to process?"

The sheriff started to respond, but Kelly motioned him aside. "She's right, sir. We'll get more out of them if we give them a little time." Kelly led him down the steps and began filling him in on what he'd observed the night before.

The sheriff and his deputies took statements from Mark, Bobby, Fred, Hunt, Ken, and Kelly.

Jimmy Two-Feathers was nowhere to be found. No one had seen him since the night before.

***

The men left the women and Hunt at the house with Dr. Melon and his family and went to search the rest of the facility. Some of it was still mostly intact, but almost every window in the place had been smashed. They checked the corpses, looking for Vandusen, and found him and Bauer, their faces set in grimaces of pain.

"Good riddance," Fred said. "They were both evil bastards."

Ken looked down at Vandusen's mutilated body. An arm and a leg had been ripped from his torso. "No one deserves to die like this, though."

Kelly led them to the building he hadn't been able to enter during his undercover work, the one where he thought the screams had come from. Sure enough, the building contained cages, strong ones, but no creatures of any kind. He kneeled to get a closer look at the wreckage of the cage doors. They'd been wrenched off from the outside. It looked like the attack had been a rescue mission.

Chris was first to speak. "Well, whatever or whoever was

216

being held in these cages is now free in the forest."

"And the attack was designed to free them," Mark said.

"Designed," Ken said thoughtfully.

They stepped outside and gazed at the dense tree line that surrounded the fence.

The sheriff looked from one to the other, a puzzled look on his face, and settled on Ken. "Dr. Turner, what exactly got loose here? And these creatures you've all mentioned—you're not seriously expecting me to believe that Bigfoot did this."

Ken shook his head. "Bigfoots didn't kill these people. They just destroyed the buildings."

"Then what did this?" He gestured to the corpses.

Before Ken could answer, the roar of two Huey helicopters interrupted, echoing off the surrounding mountains. A moment later they swooped in and hovered over the compound clearing. The group covered their eyes from the dust storm stirred up from the whirling blades. The chopper settled into silence, and several soldiers filed out.

Chris nudged Ken and whispered, "Look at the markings . . . US Army."

Fred stepped alongside and they watched several men dressed in fatigues look around as they waited for a man in plain clothes to step out.

The man smirked at them before walking toward the sheriff and asking, "Are you in charge?"

The sheriff stiffened, his gaze taking in the armed soldiers. "I am. What are you doing disturbing my crime scene?"

The man grinned. "You're out of your jurisdiction, sheriff. This is a facility of the Department of Defense, and you're trespassing on a secret facility of the US Government. Further, you're hampering duly assigned agents of the United States under Section 533 in the course of their duties. I'm ordering you to cease and desist and vacate these premises."

The soldiers pointed their M-16s toward them.

The sheriff's jaw set in a hard line, but when he observed a door gunner train a machine gun in the direction of him and the rest of the group, he motioned his men to stand down. He glared at the plainclothes man and in a loud voice declared, "I'm investigating several homicides here!"

The agent shook his head and with a smirk said, "What crime? Nothing has happened here. Sheriff, you and your men have never been here. If you report anything pertaining to your trespassing on our facility, everyone here will be arrested and detained for interrogation. You and your people are endangering the national security of the United States." He paused and nodded to a solider carrying a camera. The man began photographing them and taking their names.

***

No one spoke as they made their way back down the bumpy road that wound out of the old logging camp and back to Willow Creek. They caravaned the way they'd come—three Grand Wagoneers driven by deputy sheriffs. The sheriff sat up front in the lead vehicle, jaw clenched, staring out the passenger-side window. The agent's paperwork and credentials had been in order, so the sheriff begrudgingly had to gather his men and order them to leave.

Dr. Melon and his family rode with Mary and Sandy. Sandy made a point to ride in the front seat and listen attentively as Melon finally began sharing what had happened, beginning with his kidnapping from the university. That's how he learned that the deputy who'd so mysteriously disappeared had been murdered. Sandy's search was over, and the murderer had been punished with a gruesome death.

He found it strange that the agent had claimed he had no knowledge of Vandusen or the so-called general, but it was no longer Sandy's business. The agent made it clear that they would be undertaking their own investigation.

Consuelo and Mark took the back seat of the middle wagon with Dusty, and Tamara, Fred, and Chris shared the last deputy's wagon. Ken, Bobby, Lester, and Hunt followed Kelly to his jeep. They waited until the deputies had left before preparing to leave. Ken eyed the DOD men wandering through the carnage. He wondered how much they knew. Presumably, someone had called them in when the creatures had attacked the facility.

"Well, here we all are," Lester said as he bent over, hanging his arms down to stretch his back. "We started this whole thing together, and seems we're ending together."

"Where's that damn Indian?" Bobby said with a frown.

"He'll show up," Ken said as he dusted off his trousers. "He promised to guide us to another set of caves that he claims has all the answers we're seeking."

"Isn't this answer enough?" Kelly gestured back at the carnage. "You saw the bigfoots, and your creatures. You know where they are now." He waved his arm around, indicating the forest. "There's hundreds of miles of wilderness out there. It's not as if you'll ever have a chance of catching them again. Best leave well enough alone. Stay out their territory and hope they stay out of ours."

Ken frowned as he climbed into the front seat beside Kelly while the others squeezed into the back. *Would the DOD see it that way?* he wondered.

They hadn't gone far when the jeep skidded to a stop.

"What is it?" Ken asked. He looked up the road and could

only see dust stirred up as the caravan ahead of them dropped over a rise.

Kelly pointed at the side of the road a little way ahead. Something large moved in the shadows. Ken squinted, trying to see what it was. His question was answered a moment later when Danny and Oliver stepped out of the forest.

"Christ! Now what?" Bobby yelled.

Lester jumped out of the jeep, strode up to them and, as the others climbed cautiously out of the jeep behind him, said, "Well, old friend, you found your way to the Promised Land, I see."

Oliver tilted his head from side to side and Danny beckoned someone or something to come out of the dense forest.

A large bigfoot pushed through, breaking several low-hanging branches. The group gasped. The bigfoot stood a head taller than Oliver or Danny.

Hunt gagged from its rank smell. "Christ, that stinks!"

The bigfoot watched them warily for a moment, then beckoned back toward the forest. Six young girls stepped out from under the trees and onto the dusty road. They blinked as they looked around. When they finally saw Kelly, they burst into tears and ran to him. Kelly knelt on one knee as the girls engulfed them.

Oliver signed, "Humans safe now."

"Thank you," Ken signed back.

"We," Oliver indicated himself, Danny, and the bigfoot, "watch others."

"Others stay away now," Danny signed.

Then as silently and quickly as they'd come, Danny, Oliver, and the bigfoot disappeared back into the forest.

Lester went to follow them, but Kelly grabbed his arm and said, "We need to get these children back to what's left of their families." He fired the jeep into life.

Dusty slammed the door and said, "Let's get back to town, I'm hungry."

Lester glared at him. "Idiot."

Chapter Thirty-Seven

"A couple of the girls managed to fill us in enough for us to get the gist of it," Kelly said, looking around at the group gathered in the motel room.

Mary handed out the last of the coffees and sat on the twin bed beside Ken and Fred. Bobby sat on the floor beneath the window with Mark and Consuelo. Hunt lay on the second twin bed with Girlie, while Lester and Dusty shared the tiny sofa, and Kelly and Sandy sat on the dining chairs. Chris and Tamara sat on the floor with their backs against the ends of the beds.

"As you suspected," he continued, "the creatures killed the girls' parents and kidnapped them. They hid them in a cave but didn't harm them, though it came close. Apparently the creatures sniffed them all over, particularly"—he paused to gather himself—"between their legs. Then most of them lost interest in them, and after that a couple of them guarded them and fought any of the others who tried to go near them. They gave them a lot of food, but the girls were too terrified to try anything."

"Well, it's a relief to hear they weren't . . ." Mary trailed off.

"Harmed," Ken said, but the word he thought was *raped*. Maybe the creatures had recognized that the girls weren't yet of childbearing age.

"At one point, they all rushed out of the cave. And the girls crept out behind them. The creatures blocked the cave entrance so they couldn't escape, but they saw what they called 'the two smart ones' with a group of bigfoots, and they all seemed to be talking to each other with their hands."

"Amazing," Fred said.

Bobby whistled.

"When the two smart ones saw the girls, they got really upset. There was a lot of hooting and screeching and a fight broke out, but the bigfoots picked the fighters up, banged them together, and dropped them, stunned, on the ground."

Bobby hooted with laughter. "That's what they need, someone to keep them in line."

"Apparently, they spent a long time speaking sign language after that, and the bigfoot leader drew pictures in the sand. The creatures allowed the girls to gather around the fire where they could see what was going on, but their guard remained." Kelly paused, but no one said a thing.

Kelly nodded. "Yeah, it's pretty bizarre. Anyway, after that, most of them left, leaving six bigfoot females, two who had little babies with them. They let the girls play with the babies and sang them songs to help them sleep. They also cooked food for them, and the girls actually ate because the bigfoot were, as they said, so gentle and kind."

Ken couldn't contain his excitement. "I see my life's work taking a change in direction!"

Chris groaned. "Oh god, don't tell me you're going to be one of those Bigfoot nutters now."

Everyone chuckled, and Fred said, "Bigfoot researchers can hardly be called nutters after this gets out."

"It can't get out, though," Sandy said. "You heard the DOD

guy. None of us can talk about this."

Ken sighed. "So the existence of Bigfoot remains a mystery."

"It has to," Sandy said. He looked around at everyone. "None of you wants a visit from the DOD, do you?"

Lester held up his hands. "Not me. I'm not saying nothin'."

Everyone else nodded in agreement.

Ken sighed. "I still want to go to those caves Jimmy Two-Feathers told us about."

Several of the assembly groaned.

"Wait," Kelly said. "I haven't finished the story."

"Yes, sorry for the interruption," Ken said. "This is all just so fascinating."

"Apparently," Kelly continued, "one of the bigfoot females then gestured for the girls to follow them, and she led them to where the rest of them were gathered around some injured creatures. One of the bigfoots was healing them, and get this . . . He did it just by holding his hand over their wounds. The girls said it was like magic. One said she saw bullets popping out of them."

Bobby and Chris glanced at Hunt.

"This is getting really weird," Fred said. "Are these girls believable?"

"We interviewed the two who were up to talking to us separately," Kelly said, "but their stories matched. And they were in no state to have been able to concoct a story like that."

"Besides," Mark said, "it fits. I mean, we saw a planned, intelligent attack, and the bigfoots refraining from harming the humans directly."

Kelly nodded and continued, "Then the two smart ones and the bigfoots led the girls out. The rest you know."

"So what now?" Consuelo asked.

"My concern," Kelly said, "and the sheriff agrees, is that

even if the bigfoots really are 'gentle and kind,'"—he made quotation marks in the air with his fingers—"those creatures might massacre other campers."

"I think Oliver, Danny, and the bigfoots will prevent that," Lester said. "You all saw what they signed."

Kelly snorted. "I saw what looked like sign language, but I have no idea what it meant."

"They said the humans were safe now, that Danny, Oliver, and the bigfoots will keep an eye on the creatures," Ken said.

"You got all that from those few gestures?" Kelly queried.

Ken chuckled. "You get to see the subtleties after a while."

"The sheriff is having a hard time getting his head around all this," Kelly said. "I'm not sure he's going to believe that any of them actually talked to you."

"Communicating with primates has been the focus of Dr. Turner's research for decades now," Mary said.

Kelly nodded. "And those two are old friends who escaped when moving them between lodgings. Yeah, I know. You told me."

"Just tell him to keep the humans close to town," Dusty said. "Animals who respect each other's territory live in harmony."

Kelly smiled. "That they do. And I'll be sure to discourage anyone from heading out into bigfoot lands."

"Except for us, of course," Ken said.

Kelly stood. "No one can rescue you if you're attacked out there. Not even the DOD will be able to find those creatures."

Lester stood and offered Kelly his hand. "We'll be safe so long as Oliver and Danny are around."

Kelly shook the outstretched hand, then nodded at everyone and turned to leave.

Ken stood and accompanied him to the door. "Thanks for all your help, Ranger Kelly."

"Pleased to be of service, Dr. Turner."

The door clicked shut behind him. Ken turned and surveyed the room. For a moment no one said a word, then Ken said, "You know what this means, don't you?"

"That not only are the creatures loose in the North West of the United States," Mary said, "but also bigfoots do exist, are intelligent, have an organized society, and, if the girls weren't embellishing too much, magical healing skills. Oh, and one more thing. I'm losing my husband for another week, if not more."

Everyone laughed.

Sandy turned to Ken. "You're still planning on going to the caves with that Indian?"

Ken grinned. "Sure am."

Sandy frowned. "Why? You know they exist now, and it's not as if you can release any research on any of this."

Ken chuckled. "Proof that something exists is not enough for a scientist. We want to know how they exist, what kind of culture they have, if any. In this case, and, perhaps most important, where they come from."

"If only for our own edification," Fred added.

Hunt sat up. "I'm coming."

"Those caves are a couple of days' hike into difficult terrain," Chris said. "Are you sure you're up to it?"

Hunt nodded. "I can do it, and my mind's made up. You'll not change it. Those bigfoots were amazing, truly gentle giants. I want to see another one, if it's the last thing I do," he declared.

Chris stood. "Well, I have to get back. I have animals to organize for another movie."

"And I have a murder investigation to close," Sandy said.

"Since it's all being kept hush-hush," Dusty said, "Girlie, Oliver, and Danny won't be arrested for protecting us from Vandusen's thugs?" He glanced at Lester. "Or us for helping?"

Sandy nodded. "Yeah. Don't worry about that."

"And I should get back to work," Tamara said. "Do you think we're safe now?"

"Why would the DOD bother with us anymore?" Fred said. "We assured them we won't talk. Their facility is unusable and the hybrids unreachable. If they still want to pursue this idea, they'll have to start from scratch."

"We don't even have Danny and Oliver anymore," Ken said.

"And I think their investigation of what happened at their facility will keep them busy for a while."

"And just in case," Bobby said with a grin and an evil gleam in his eyes, "someone should write a book about all this." He glanced at Tamara. "A manuscript that we could have hidden away and could threaten to release to the media, should any of us find ourselves hassled by any other creeps this general or any of his cronies might send our way."

"Several manuscripts," Chris said.

"And a screenplay," Dusty added.

They all laughed.

The phone rang.

Mary picked it up. "A message for Lt. Sandy," she said, holding out the phone. "From your office."

While the rest of the crew went to their own rooms, Sandy nodded at the phone and took down some details. "It's from François," he said when he'd replaced the receiver. "I have to find a radio tower. The ranger service should have one."

Chapter Thirty-Eight

François smiled at the radioman. He thought of saying something about the radio conversation he'd had with Sandy but thought better of it. He realized this was a change for him, this being so talkative. He'd always preferred to keep his thoughts to himself, which had served him well throughout his career. But lately, he had the surprising desire to share his thoughts with almost anyone who would listen. It was as though he was trying to make sense of what had happened since Dr. Turner and his company stumbled onto their facility. *How long has it been?*

He stepped out onto the porch overlooking their new compound and was pleased with what he saw. His men had been busy. They had worked with energy, trying to finish everything before the rainy season. That was on top of doing weekly patrols deep into the jungle, searching for the creatures who'd managed to escape when Vandusen and his gangsters had set them loose during the raid on their old place.

The radioman nodded and said, "Message coming through."

François started to say something, but the radioman held his hand up as he wrote frantically. "Wow! That operator sure sends fast!"

In seconds he held the transcribed message.

"Been in touch with Bobby and crew STOP. Group received message STOP. Sending congratulations STOP. We are in a new chapter now STOP. Will join you ASAP STOP. Send list of what you need STOP."

François read the message several times. Turner and his group were not going to abandon him. They would come to his aid. He smiled at the thought of seeing Lester again. They'd grown close, and of course, there was Girlie.

The radioman heard François laughing and looked up from adjusting the dials.

Chapter Thirty-Nine

Ken stood at the opening of the cave and peered into the darkness. Bobby, Hunt, Mark, and Fred gathered around him. It looked as though Ken was about to be swallowed by the black gaping mouth of the cave. He turned to the rest and hesitated before saying, "So . . . let's take a look."

"You first," Bobby said, leaning forward trying to get a better look. "Who has flashlights?"

Ken held one up, and Fred pulled one from a side pocket of his pack. Hunt and Mark followed his lead.

"I've got one in here somewhere," Bobby said, rummaging through his backpack. "Where's Sandy when we need him?" he asked no one in particular.

Hunt laughed nervously. "You know, a cop is never around when you need one." He leaned over his knees, trying to catch his breath.

Ken waited until Bobby found his flashlight and Hunt stood upright. "Okay, let's get going." He stepped into the darkness.

"Hold up! Where the fuck is Jimmy?" Bobby asked, his voice higher pitched than usual.

No one answered as they all looked back the way they'd come. Jimmy Two-Feathers was gone.

"Where the hell's he gone to now?" Fred pulled out a hatchet from his pack.

Ken shook his head. "So what? He'd just chant and speak in riddles." He motioned them to follow him as he dissolved into the darkness.

It took several minutes to orient themselves in the pitch black of the cave. They could hear drips echoing off a ceiling they couldn't see. The darkness swallowed them despite their flashlights. Suddenly bats swirled around their heads. Ken ducked. Bobby yelled and dropped his flashlight, covering his head with his hands. Ken stared after them, shining his flashlight on their retreating forms. He guessed, by the bats high-pitched squeaks, that they were flying out of the cave. Bobby regained his composure, passed Ken, and led them down further into the darkness. Occasionally he stopped to listen, but always they continued their trek downward into the bowels of the rock.

After what seemed like an eternity, they stepped into an open gallery so enormous that it swallowed their flashlights. They could barely make out the ceiling, but their flashlights lit the walls.

Hunt called them over to a high, smooth part. "Take a look at this."

They gathered around him and pointed their flashlights onto the pale gray limestone wall.

Hunt pulled out a handkerchief to cover his mouth, and after a fit of coughing, said, "Damn, we need more light."

A voice in the darkness startled them. "Maybe this will help."

They shaded their eyes against a Coleman Lantern as it hissed into life. Jimmy Two-Feathers stood behind, holding it. He motioned Hunt to take two more he held in his other hand. "Here, light these."

The flickering light revealed an enormous wall of cave

drawings. The group stared at it in silent awe.

"This is the creation tale of the Hupa—my people," Jimmy said in a wistful whisper. The huge gallery echoed with the hissing and sputtering of the lanterns.

Hunt walked up close to the wall and leaned back to take in the giant petroglyphs of six tall, humanlike figures, with two more above them. The figures appeared to gaze up into the sky at two round orbs with wavy rays emitting from their centers. A carved moon sat low on the horizon beside two peaks.

"My people know those peaks. They're sacred." Jimmy set down his lantern, raised his arms, and chanted in a language they didn't understand.

The figures seemed to dance with the flickering of the lanterns. Hundreds of drawings filled the wall. Some were carved deep in the limestone, while others had been painted in a staggering array of colors.

"This must be a very secret and sacred place," Mark whispered.

The rest of the team looked at one another and nodded.

"What does this mean?" Ken asked, lightly tracing his finger in the air over the tall figures.

Pointing at the six figures, Jimmy said, "It tells how the Ohmah, Bigfoot as you White people call him, came to be in our forest."

"And these two?" Ken asked.

"Their leaders," Jimmy replied. "See how they are placed over the other six?"

"That's it!" Bobby's voice bounced off the walls, startling all of them. "Two over six—it makes sense now."

"Ah, yes." Fred walked back and forth along the drawings, then pointed at the two orbs and counted each of the figures in the air. "Remember the rows of flies in Danny's cage that almost got me killed? I can't help but think that Danny and Oliver are somehow related to all this. To Bigfoot."

"Perhaps both are results of the early Soviet experiments," Ken said.

Fred stepped closer. "The moon in the petroglyph is full, and its position next to these peaks could give us the year this supposedly happened, or at least, the time of the year. Being there at the right time might be illuminating, to say the least . . ." He turned to Jimmy Two-Feathers. "The moon is full tomorrow, isn't it?"

Jimmy nodded.

"Can you lead us to these peaks?" Fred asked. "To the place where the artist stood to see this?" He waved his arm at the painting.

"The Maiden comes to visit that place at the solstices." Jimmy's lips moved in whispers, apparently counting. "That is tomorrow evening. I can lead you there, but we will first have to purify ourselves and be worthy of that journey, and we will need to hurry, or you will have to wait another year." Jimmy took a long raven feather from his hat and waved it around, casting dark dancing shadows against the cave walls.

***

The group stepped out of the cave entrance into an evening which felt balmy compared to the chill of the caves. The tops of the trees swayed to a faint, whispering breeze. Their crowns opened to a cloudless sky that framed the dust of stars making up the Milky Way. They twinkled their different colors and seemed near enough to touch. Without a word, the group followed Jimmy Two-Feathers back down the path on which they'd come.

"We can camp here for the night," he said when they came to a level site. "And if we leave early,"—he glanced at Hunt—

"we will be able to get to that place in time to see the moon, same as in the painting."

The next day, they traveled slowly, with plenty of rest stops for Hunt. Jimmy led them on a winding game trail beneath giant trees and through countless meadows and glens. Eventually, they came into an open river valley where the roar of a nearby stream racing over the shallows of the glen made it hard to engage in conversation, if any had been inclined. They traveled silently, all feeling that they were racing toward an ending but without any idea of what it would look like. So they just kept hiking.

Just at dusk, they reached several large, smooth boulders that seemed out of place among the tall meadow grasses. An alluvial skirt fanned up the slopes toward two peaks, jagged against the brightening glow of the moon as it rose behind the distant ridges.

"It won't be long now. The Maiden will visit us soon, and then we'll see," Jimmy whispered almost in a song.

Ken motioned all to stay among the boulders and wait. He wondered what would happen next. The moonlight grew so bright that it reflected off the smooth white boulders and cast them in shadow. Except for blasts high up in the treetops, all remained quiet and still. Nothing moved in the open surrounding them.

They saw more as the moon cleared the crags beside the two peaks, seeming to grow in size and brightness as it rose toward its place in the painting. Ken pointed at a pack of coyotes who slid silently through the grass. They stopped and sat watching. A raven landed on a manzanita bush almost within reach of Jimmy and, without a croak, tilted its head from side to side toward the rising moon. A herd of elk stood at the edge of the woods, noses pointed in the direction of the peaks.

"The witnesses are gathering," Jimmy said, nodding toward

the animals.

When the moon reached the place in the eastern sky recorded in the painting, two bright, shining orbs appeared high overhead.

The humans' eyes widened, and some shook their heads in disbelief. Though none spoke, they all recognized the orbs as something not of their world.

Bobby frowned and tapped Hunt on the arm. When he turned, Bobby mouthed a query, "Spaceships?"

Hunt shrugged.

The coyotes howled, and Jimmy began to dance and chant to their chorus. A shrill song from above filled the air. As though summoned, a band of large creatures crossed the river and made their way to the foot of the peaks.

No one moved as they watched the creatures gather silently at the edge of the woods and gaze at the rising moon. Six large creatures split off from the rest of the troop and made their way up the alluvia toward the peaks. A large bear splashed across the stream and paused in the middle to watch the creatures. The hoots of an owl could just be heard above the whitewater. A cougar slunk out of the shadows and lay in the plush grass, tail twitching. The moon filled the eastern sky so brightly that the humans had to shade their eyes, all except Jimmy Two-Feathers. He walked toward the conclave of animals, singing in words they didn't comprehend, but images visited them just the same. Images of tall, adorned humanlike creatures descending to earth from the orbs in the starlit sky.

Suddenly, a chorus of hoots and whistles rose up from the glen as the two orbs grew blindingly bright. They burned bright crimson like the celestial flames of the birth of two stars. None of the creatures moved as the six approached the rising moon and searing orbs. Soon they stood under the glowing orbs and beckoned toward the shadows of the forest. Two figures nearly as tall as the bigfoots stepped out of the tree line and joined the six.

Ken glanced at Lester for confirmation. He nodded and mouthed, "Danny and Oliver."

The whole forest shimmered and glowed, intensifying as the two greeted the six. From deep in the surrounding forest rose the greeting songs of those gathering—bigfoots and creatures alike—and as though in answer, a blinding burst of light shot from the suspended orbs and washed over all creatures, humans, and animals alike.

An overwhelming feeling of contentment and safety washed over the group and remained even after the light had extinguished, leaving the meadow to bask once more in the moonlight.

To their amazement, the glen was empty except for them.

Ken opened his mouth to say that maybe bigfoots hadn't come from the Soviet experiments, but he couldn't bring himself to voice what he figured they all suspected after witnessing those orbs and what might have been some form of communication. He motioned everyone to follow him back the way they'd come. Hunt trailed them as he struggled to keep his footing in the deep grass of the meadow. While they noticed Hunt falling further behind, no one could bring themselves to say anything. Without a word, Bobby dropped back to walk alongside his friend.

"Don't wait for me. I'll catch up." Hunt kneeled, gasping for air.

Bobby gently patted Hunt on his back and handed him a canteen. "No worries, amigo. I'm in no hurry. Take your time. Hell, I'm tired too."

Hunt gave him a sideways glance before saying, "I mean it. You're going to lose the rest and end up lost."

"Not likely." Bobby pointed at the group, who were

backtracking toward them.

Ignoring them, Hunt removed his bandanna from his neck to wet it, which revealed a purple, dime-sized lesion on his neck, jagged on the edges and oozing. They glanced at each other knowingly.

When the others arrived, Ken broke the silence, saying, "We'll make camp here for the night. Someone gather firewood. It's going to get chilly if the mist returns."

Fred took off, happy to have something to do. Ken watched him until he disappeared into the woods. He thought of yelling for him to stay in sight but knew it would do no good. He remembered another time in Africa when Bobby had done the same. He could see the concern on everyone's faces as they watched Hunt lean back against a tree and close his eyes. Fortunately, his breathing was slowing back to normal.

When Fred stepped back out of the undergrowth carrying a bundle of firewood, a dark shadow stepped out behind him.

"What?" Fred asked when he noticed them staring in his direction.

Mark pointed and nodded, indicating something behind him.

Fred turned and, eyes wide, dropped the sticks at the sight of a large bigfoot gliding up from behind him.

Long amber hair that was matted and tangled covered the bigfoot, who stood a head taller than Ken, the tallest among them. He had piercing, alert eyes and arms that hung almost to his knees.

The bigfoot passed Fred and stopped in front of Bobby and Hunt. It ignored all of them except for Hunt, who had his eyes closed. Bobby stepped protectively in front of Hunt, but before he could say or do anything, the creature held his hand up, palm toward him. Bobby glanced at the rest of the group before he held his hand up in response. The bigfoot tilted its head from side to side, then kneeled next to Hunt.

A foul smell assaulted the group, reminiscent of dirty diapers. Several pulled out their handkerchiefs and covered their noses. A closer look by the group revealed that the bigfoot was a male. The group backed away, except for Bobby, who stood his ground, but they relaxed when the bigfoot gently stroked Hunt's cheek. Hunt smiled, appearing to be asleep.

That was when it happened. A light grew from Hunt's cheek and spread over his whole body until its intensity was so bright that the group had to shade their eyes. A hum rose up from the surrounding forest and vibrated the ground around them. Soon only the glowing images of the bigfoot and Hunt could be seen. Hunt stood and embraced the creature. A burst of flames exploded, blinding the watchers. When their sight returned, Hunt was standing alone, looking down at Bobby, who uncovered his eyes.

"Sorry," Hunt said, "I guess I fainted." He gathered his belongings, which lay strewn on the ground, pausing with a frown when he realized the rest of the group all stood staring at him, mouths agape. "What's wrong with you all? I'm okay now." He bounded down the trail, motioning them to follow him.

Bobby had to run to catch up with him. "Wait! You need to conserve your energy. We've a long way yet to go. Don't you want to set up camp?"

Without halting, Hunt looked over his shoulder and said, "I feel great, and there are better campsites further down, right Jimmy?" He almost ran down the path, motioning them to follow.

Jimmy nodded. "He's right, there are better places to camp within just another hour's walk."

The group looked at one another, unable to speak. Bobby finally broke the silence. "You heard the man. Let's get going.

The moon will light our way."

They gathered their belongings and set out to catch up to Hunt. Bobby whispered to Ken, "Did you notice? His lesion is gone."

Nodding, Ken said, "The girls weren't embellishing." His eyes followed Hunt up the trail. "It's time we headed back to Reno. We've a primate center to run," he said before he struck out.

Hunt looked back over his shoulder and yelled, "And don't forget what Mary shared with us. I think we're needed in Africa too."

***

The bigfoot rejoined the rest of his group. They'd observed him helping the humans and watched the previously sick human lead the rest of his kind up the trail and out of their country. Several of his companions pushed in around him as they looked from their leader to the humans far below. They made room for two of the creatures who had invaded their homeland.

Danny and Oliver pointed at the humans and signed, "Friend."

The bigfoot leader looked Danny and Oliver up and down, then grimaced before he signaled his troop to follow him back into the Trinity forest.

Danny and Oliver watched them fade into the old-growth trees like spirits.

Oliver signed, "Go now." Both turned and followed Hunt and the rest up the trail.

A Note from the Author

It would be immensely helpful to me if you could write a review for *Beyond Human* and publish it at your point of purchase. I need your reviews to help find the readers who will enjoy my work.

Also, please sign up to my newsletter and receive some true stories of my life with chimps, for free. Find out more by visiting my website at http://bajamotoquest.com.

And please stay in touch:

Follow @KenDecroo on Twitter
Like Ken Decroo on Facebook

Acknowledgments

The journey of writing a novel is long and winding. There are so many humans and nonhumans to thank. The characters of this series are based on my experiences in the world of wild animal training and research. I am grateful to have worked with many unique people and lived in the company of chimpanzees and other wild animals. They have taught me a lot about humility and love. I thank them all.

This book has evolved and grown as a result of the mentoring and guidance of my world-class editor, Tahlia Newland of AIA Publishing. The book covers in this series were created by Rose Newland. I would like to thank AIA Publishing for taking a chance on another of my books.

Instrumental in this series were: the Playa de Estero people, Rosemary Douglas Kelley and Mike Kelley, Steve and Dorothy Clark, Kathryn Lynn Davis and her writers' group, Ken and Lois Decroo, Jamie Stortz Morris, Joanne Larsen, Brad and Vicki Throgmorton for their hospitality in Willow Creek, Tracy Lenocker PE, WM6T, for his HAM radio expertise, and Tamara Lynn Decroo. Most importantly, I would like to thank my readers and followers.

About the Author

Kenneth L. Decroo truly believes you must live a life worth writing about. Before he became an educator and consultant for universities and school districts, he worked in the world of research and wild animal training in the motion picture industry for many years. He holds advance degrees in anthropology, instructional technology, and education. He lives and writes between his ranch (the Lazy D) in Tarpley, Texas, and in the San Bernardino mountains of Southern California with his wife, Tammy. When not writing and lecturing, he loves to ride his BMW adventure motorcycle down the Baja peninsula to beaches and bays without names. More about his adventures can be found on his blog, http://bajamotoquest.com.